For Alison,
*mia moglie*

# Contents

*You cannot express the passion of joy with a short tail.*

— Mark Twain, "A Cat Tale"

# Prologue: Bones in the Yard

♦ ♦ ♦ ♦ ♦ ♦ ♦ ♦ ♦ ♦

**Oobroorr gurr yurr** *(Bowwow): A lot of bones have been buried in the yard*

Much has happened since I finished my first story, dear reader, or, as we electric dogs like to say, *Oobroorr gurr yurr.* So much has happened, in fact, that as I sit here poised, pen in mouth, ready to set it all down, I find that I am not sure where to begin. The temptation is to cut to the chase — to the rocket rides and the parachuting dogs, to the coyote pack and the blue desert cat, to the trips around the world. But I should go carefully. I mustn't let the story get away from me. I mustn't let the tale wag the dog.

I suppose I will just begin at the beginning. That's always a good place to start. I'll dig up a bone at a time, dust each one off, and give each a thorough gnawing over. Then, when they have all been unearthed, and well-savored, the story will be complete.

Now, you shouldn't worry, gentle reader, if you don't know — or can't remember — what happened in the first story. You'll find out everything you'll need to know — including all about electric dogs, and even electric girls — once the bones start coming up. Bark of honor.

So, what do you say — shall we begin digging?

# Enough

♦ ♦ ♦ ♦ ♦ ♦ ♦

# 1

"What's this?" my master Faith said when I set the manuscript of my first story on her lap. *"Faith and the Electric Dogs,"* she read. Her freckled cheeks blushed. "I like the title."

My tail pounded on the mattress.

As she thumbed through the pages, strands of her bright orange hair slipped out from her blue Guatemalan hairband and fell down into her eyes. She brushed them away. They fell back down. She brushed them away again, over and over. Over and over, they fell back into her eyes. From time to time, she blew the loosened hairs upward. This also had no lasting effect.

"Oh, Eddie!" she squealed finally. "It's about *us*!" She reached over and gave my brisket a rub.

I leaned into it. I adore brisket rubs. But then, just as it was getting good, she jumped down from the bed.

"Let's show Mama!" she said excitedly. "This will change her mind about you!"

I wasn't so sure about that. Faith's mother, Bernice, had never really taken a shine to me. I can't say why, exactly, other than, perhaps, that I'm a dog. Some people have a thing against dogs. Especially electric ones.

We found Bernice in the kitchen, in a chair at the table, her face in her hands. Hector, her husband and Faith's *padrastro*, stood behind her, rubbing her shoulders.

**padrastro** *(Spanish): stepfather*

I smelled trouble. To be on the safe side, I scooted under the cooking table — the one with the *estufa* on top of it.

**estufa** *(Spanish): stove*

"Here's Faith," Hector murmured. "Let's tell her now."

Bernice lowered her hands. A strand of dull orange hair drooped into her eyes. She brushed it away. It fell back.

"Mama!" Faith said, rushing up to her. "Edison wrote a story!"

"Oh, not now, Faith!" Bernice said wearily.

"But, Mama!" Faith said. "Look!" She held up the manuscript for Bernice to see.

"I don't have time for foolishness!" Bernice said, blowing her hair out of her face. It drooped back into her eyes. "We need to talk to you about something very important!"

*"Mi hija,"* Hector said to Faith, "I just got a phone call from the university in the States. They have a teaching position for me and want me to come immediately."

**mi hija** ***(Spanish): an affectionate term for a little girl; literally, my daughter***

"We leave Mexico tomorrow night," Bernice said. "We're going home."

"What?" Faith gasped. "What do you mean? We *are* home!"

"I mean *home* home!" Bernice said. "To San Francisco!"

"But I don't want to go!" Faith whined.

"You don't want to go?" Bernice said. "Before you were begging to!"

"I know," Faith said, frowning. "But I like it here now."

Bernice heaved a sigh. "I know, sweetheart," she said. "I'm sorry. I'm not too happy about it myself."

"What about Eddie?" Faith asked suddenly. I pricked up my ears.

"No!" Bernice said. She waved a finger at me cowering under the *estufa*. I was surprised she had noticed I was there. "That dog stays here!"

"But, Mama!" Faith said, beginning to cry.

"Oh, Bernice," Hector said.

*"Grumph groomph,"* I grumbled.

**Grumph groomph** ***(Bowwow): I'm not surprised***

"No!" Bernice said again. "No dog!"

"But what about his *story*?" Faith pleaded. She plopped the manuscript down on Bernice's lap.

Bernice sprang to her feet, launching my story into the air. The pages burst into a cloud of fluttering paper.

*"¡Basta!"* she shrieked. She stomped her foot. "No dog! That's final!"

**¡Basta!** ***(Spanish): Enough!***

For a tense moment, the three of them just stood silently, the pages of my story settling down over them. Then, bravely, Hector spoke. "What are you suggesting we do with him?" he said.

Bernice squinted at him. "I'm sure the Paniaguas will take him," she said. "They like dogs."

The Paniaguas? *¿Pan y agua?* Was that to be my future?

**¿Pan y agua?**
***(Spanish): bread and water***

"In fact, I'll call them right now," Bernice said and walked to the phone.

Hector knelt in front of Faith. "I'm so sorry, *mi hija,*" he said softly.

Faith just stared at her shoes. She was sulking. It's sort of a habit of hers. I ran over to her and licked at her fingers. This revived her.

"Come on!" she said suddenly, and then skipped from the room. I followed along, of course. That's what good dogs do.

"*¡Buenas tardes, Señor Paniagua!*" Bernice said cheerfully into the phone as we passed.

**¡Buenas tardes, Señor Paniagua!**
***(Spanish): Good afternoon, Mr. Paniagua!***

Faith plucked a glittery purple pencil from her pencil cup in her room, then raced back to the kitchen. She stood in the doorway and waited for Bernice to finish her call. I waited with her. Such a good dog.

**¿La raza?**
*(Spanish): The breed?*

**corriente**
*(Spanish): common; also, current, as in electrical current*

**Un perro corriente**
*(Spanish): a mutt; literally, a common dog; can also be translated as "an electric dog"*

*"¿La raza?"* Bernice asked into the phone. She looked over at me. At that particular moment, I was biting my right rear paw for absolutely no reason at all. *"Corriente,"* she said with a sigh.

*"¿Un perro corriente?"* Señor Paniagua's voice groaned from the earpiece. His laughter could be heard clear across the room. The Paniaguas like dogs, I gathered, so long as they aren't electric.

Deflated, and more than a little perturbed, Bernice thanked Señor Paniagua for his time and hung up the phone.

"Mama," Faith said firmly, marching up to her mother. "Eddie's going with!" She stomped her foot. "That's final!"

I ducked. I whimpered. I wished I had stayed under the *estufa*.

But then, before Bernice could react, Faith leaned over and wagged the pencil in front of my snout.

"Go ahead, Eddie," she said. "Show her!"

Bernice closed her eyes and pressed her fingertips to them. "Oh, for Pete's sake," she said.

Hector clapped his hands. "Oh, Faith! You are so *chistosa*!"

**chistosa** *(Spanish): funny*

"Go on," Faith whispered to me. She rubbed my brisket. She knows how to get her way.

I took the pencil in my mouth and pulled a stray sheet of the manuscript closer. When I set the graphite tip to it, I heard Bernice gasp. Hector, too.

"That's it," Faith whispered. "Show 'em."

But I couldn't. Not a single word came to my mind. Pressure can be so stifling.

"Okay, that's it!" Bernice said. "I've had enough of this nonsense! More than enough!"

And then I had it.

With both question marks, one right side up, the other upside down, I wrote *¿Basta?*

# Applesauce

♦ ♦ ♦ ♦ ♦ ♦ ♦ ♦ ♦

# 2

**querida** ***(Spanish): sweetheart; dear***

"No," Bernice said again.

*"Querida,"* Hector said. "We have to."

"No!" Bernice said, and slammed her suitcase shut. She tried to latch it, but it was stuffed too full. "Oh, for crying out loud," she grumbled, and stepped up onto the bed. She sat down on the suitcase and pounded at the latch with her fist.

"Bernice," Hector said in a low tone. "You saw what he can do."

He looked over at me lying by Faith in the bedroom doorway, gnawing the glittery purple pencil.

"We have to take him with us," Hector said. "He — he is not as electric as we thought!"

Bernice jumped down from the suitcase. "It's a

physical impossibility!" she yelled, waving her arms about like some great bird. "Do you really think that we can just bring a dog into the United States, just like that? Without shots? Without papers? It can't be done! There isn't time!"

Her emotion burned so hot that the scent of her tea tree oil made my eyes water. (She dabs it behind her ears every morning.)

"I'll take him to Dr. Zarpas in the morning," Hector said.

"You don't understand!" Bernice said wildly. "Don't you know what will happen to our lives if word of this were ever to get out?" Her eyes bugged. "Pandemonium! Sheer and utter pandemonium! The world will be at our doorstep! The circus will come to town!"

"The circus?" Faith whispered to me. "What's she talking about?"

I didn't have a clue.

"Bernice," Hector said seriously. "The dog is literate."

Bernice sunk back onto the bed. She brought

her hand up and covered her eyes. Hector sat down beside her.

"Don't worry," he said, putting his arm around her. "It'll be all right."

Bernice sniffled. "Oh, right!" she said. "I'm sure everything will be just swell!"

"Let's read the story!" Faith said, clapping her hands.

"Absolutely not!" Bernice said. "We have too much to do!"

"Oh, *querida*," Hector said.

"Come on, Mama," Faith said. "It's all about us. All of us." Then she turned to me. "Isn't it, widdle puppler wuppler?"

"Widdle," "puppler," and "wuppler" are words from a language that Faith apparently developed herself. I've taken to calling it Widdlish. She only speaks it to non-human animals, though I have on occasion heard her use it with Bernice or Hector, especially when she wants something.

"I'm going to pack," Bernice answered, and climbed back onto her suitcase. "I suggest you do the same."

Faith raised her eyebrows at Hector as if to say, "Well?"

♦ ♦ ♦

Faith lay on her back on the big circular handwoven rug in the *sala* and I stretched out perpendicularly to her, with my chin on her belly. Hector sat down on the sofa with the reconstructed manuscript in his lap.

**sala** *(Spanish): living room*

"It's in English," he said.

"I saw some Spanish, too," Faith said.

"You haven't read it yet?" Hector asked.

"No, Eddie just showed —" Faith began, when Bernice suddenly stepped into the room. She had on her fuzzy blue bathrobe and slippers and had her hair tied back with a ribbon. On her face she had slathered cold cream to the point that only her eyes, nostrils, and lips remained visible. Without a word, she strode past us to the stuffed chair beside the sofa, and sat. The three of us just gaped at her until finally she stomped her foot and said, "Read!"

Hector cleared his throat. *"Faith and the Electric Dogs,"* he read.

"Good title," Faith said, wriggling a little under my chin.

Hector turned the page and began the story much as he would any story. Only it wasn't just any story. It was our story — of how Faith and I met, how I came to live with the family, how Faith and I went on a rocket adventure. I loved hearing Hector read it. Especially when he laughed. Or Faith did and my head bounced.

Bernice never laughed. She never even smiled. I wondered if she even was listening. She just filed her nails, then brushed her hair, then polished her nails. At one point, she picked up a magazine and flipped through it.

But then Hector read this passage from Chapter 8:

> "Edison!" Bernice yelled. "Edison!"
>
> I pulled my head in.
>
> "Keep your head in the car," she barked.

She had Faith roll up my window so that all I could do was press my snout up against the glass.

Bernice stood suddenly and left the room.

*"¿Querida?"* Hector called after her.

She didn't answer.

A few minutes later she returned and stomped over to an upright chair in the far, darkened corner. She drew her legs up beneath her, brought her hand up to her mouth, and chewed her fingernails. She gave Hector a withering glance and he continued:

Neither Faith nor I spoke as we drove toward town. Bernice just scowled and grumbled.

Hector glanced nervously at his wife in the dark corner.

"Go on!" she snapped.

In Chapter 12, "Blast Off," Faith's rocket, the *Peahen*, did.

*"¡Mi hija!"* Hector exclaimed. "Is this true? Did it fly?"

"I told you!" Faith said. "You guys didn't believe me when I told you that Eddie and I flew in the *Peahen* and landed on an island with a bunch of electric dogs —"

"Oh, Faith!" Bernice groaned. "I don't want to hear all that rocket nonsense again!"

"But it's *true*!" Faith whined.

"Where is the rocket?" Hector asked Faith.

Bernice groaned again.

"Probably where we left her," Faith replied.

I hadn't thought about that. Maybe she was still out there.

"Applesauce," Bernice mumbled over in the corner. "It's a physical impossibility."

Bernice had a lot to learn about the realm of the possible. And she would. Firsthand.

Several chapters later, Hector held up the page he was reading so I could see it, and asked, "How do you pronounce this word?" He pointed at the Bowwow word for "bone."

**oor**
***(Bowwow):***
***bone***

*"'Oor,'"* I answered.

*"'Oor,'"* Faith repeated. "Like that?"

She didn't pronounce it in nearly a growly enough voice, and she definitely spoke with a human accent, but all in all it was a fair approximation — a nice try. So I nodded.

"I want to learn a dog language," she said matter-of-factly.

*"Oor,"* Hector said, passably.

Then finally, hours after he'd begun, Hector read the last page:

> And then, once my abilities had developed to a level which I felt were suitable for doing so, I wrote a whole story, from beginning to end. A true story, about Faith and me and the electric dogs.
>
> I hope you liked it.
>
> the end

Faith nuzzled her face into my dewlap, and said, in Widdlish, "Oh, moochy poochly-poo!"

Hector leaned forward and gave me a hearty scratch between the ears.

Bernice rose from her chair, her face hidden in cream and shadows. "Good night," she said, and went off to bed.

# The Last Day

♦ ♦ ♦ ♦ ♦ ♦ ♦ ♦ ♦ ♦ ♦ ♦ ♦

# 3

"I don't want to go," Faith muttered as she tugged on a pair of purple stockings.

"Come on, pumpkin," Bernice said, opening Faith's *armario*. "Get dressed. It's your last day."

**armario** ***(Spanish): armoire; wardrobe***

She rooted around for a suitable pair of shoes for her daughter to wear on her final day of school in Mexico. Instead, she found me, lying among the footwear, chewing on the tongue of a heavy black leather boot. She hissed and tore it from my grasp.

"Do they know I'm moving away?" Faith asked, taking the boot and slipping it onto her purple right foot.

"Yes," Bernice said, trying to wrest the boot's mate out from under my hindquarters. "I called — *umph!* I'm sure Señora Tiza — *umph* —

will have some kind of good-bye — *umph* — planned." I rose up off the boot and Bernice tumbled over backward onto the floor.

**Grumph muroo** *(Bowwow): I'm sorry*

*"Grumph muroo,"* I said.

I tagged along while Faith was clothed and fed and put into Hector's truck. Then Hector turned to me and said, "Come on, Edison. After I drop off Faith, I'm taking you to Dr. Zarpas."

Now, ordinarily, I am not one to rush at the invitation of a trip to the vet. But this time I rushed. I like riding with Hector. He lets me stick my head out the window.

Dr. Zarpas probed me and pricked me and investigated parts of my body I wouldn't have thought he'd want to. (What makes a human being decide to be a veterinarian anyway?) Then he gave Hector a signed certificate and a small brown glass bottle filled with pills. Hector purchased a large plastic box with a hinged metal grate at one end and a handle on the top. It looked like some sort of *equipaje*. A kennel, he called it. He tossed it in the back of the truck and we headed for home. The wind blew my ears back.

**equipaje** *(Spanish): luggage*

At home, Bernice feverishly guided Hector through the house, saying "That can stay," or "That needs to go," or "What on earth do we need that for?" I did my best to just stay out of the way. I had no real belongings anyway, save for my story and the bones buried in the garden. I rooted one of them up and lay in Bernice's fuchsia bed, gnawing. Gnawing helps me think. Soon I fell asleep, and began to dream.

I was running very fast, faster than I had ever run. I guess I was chasing something, or something was chasing me. And then suddenly I was falling. I don't know why. I just was. Dreams are like that. My legs scrambled madly in the air, fruitlessly searching for a pawhold. Below me, clouds drifted by! Birds swirled around my head! An airplane roared past!

"Edison!" a voice from beside me called. "Edison!"

It was Hector.

"Are you okay? You were really yowling."

I sat up. I was still in the fuchsias.

"Were you dreaming you were running?" he

asked with a smile. "Your paws were waving in the air."

Then, inexplicably, I was seized by a great urge to be out on the street — to be free. I leapt from the fuchsia bed and ran around and around the peach trees, my doghouse, Hector. I ran to the gate and scratched and whined.

**Hoo-hoooooo!** *(Bowwow): Let me out!*

*"Hoo-hoooooo!"* I cried. *"Hoo-hoooooo!"*

**Cálmate** *(Spanish): Calm down*

*"Cálmate, cálmate,"* Hector said, coming over. "You can go out." He opened the gate and I raced out onto the cobblestones of Avenida Pichucalco. "Just be home before the rains start!" he called after me.

Hector was not remiss, dear reader, in letting me out. Faith had argued several months earlier that I should be allowed to go out sometimes and visit my old street pals. It was cruel, she said, to keep me from my friends, and, besides, I was up-to-date on my shots.

My senses became unusually acute as I coursed the familiar streets of San Cristóbal de las Casas. I think I was just instinctually storing up the smells, sounds, and sights of home for later, for San Francisco, when I might wish to remember, say, the precise perfume of the pine needles that covered the street after a *boda*, or the sound of the bare feet of *niños* running over the cobblestones.

**boda** *(Spanish): wedding*

**niños** *(Spanish): children*

I noted the unremarkable place of my birth — a seldom-used doorway over on Avenida 5 de Mayo. The turquoise paint on the door was peeling away, revealing yellow beneath. I sniffed around, hoping traces of my family had somehow remained. They hadn't.

I noted also the spot on Avenida General Utrilla where I had once been run down by a taxicab. Had it not been for Faith coming along just then as she did, I should probably have died right there. Instead, I became a house dog. I sniffed the sidewalk and found an old, dried-up spot of blood. I licked it. It was mine.

And then I came to the cathedral, where Furf, my mother, went to die. The parvovirus had gotten into her, as it had to so many of my kind, and had taken its usual ghastly toll. She had managed somehow, in the final moments of her life, to stagger unnoticed through the cathedral's open doors. Later, two men carried her out, her body wrapped in a blanket.

I wasn't with her that day. Once she knew she had parvo, she shunned me and the rest of the litter. I think she was just afraid that the virus would leap to us, like fleas. When I finally learned of her death, it was from word on the street.

"That's just the way it is out here," Mark, the dog who told me, said. "If the taxis don't get you, the parvo surely will."

Mark himself died just a few months ago. Parvovirus.

I climbed the steps to the cathedral. The doors were open. I smelled candle smoke and cedar, but nothing of my mother.

"Grumph!" someone barked from behind me.

I turned around to see a pack of street dogs hunkering past, all skin and bones and despair.

"Grumph!" I heard again.

Grumph, dear reader, is my Bowwow name. Faith named me Edison. Furf named me Grumph.

Yip's scent preceded him. I followed my nose to one of the most true-blue, dyed-in-the-wool mutts I know — a real dog. We circled and did those things people would never do when they meet. (I'm sure you've seen dogs do this, dear reader, and know just where it is we put our snouts.)

"So, Grumph old boy," Yip said with a nudge. "How's things on the inside?"

Yip is electric, too, and except for being much thinner, bears a striking resemblance to myself. He's tan and short haired and houndy. He has droopy ears, a whiplike tail, and the characteristic creased brow that gives us San Cristóbal de las Casas electric dogs our woeful air. His eyes, however, are green. Mine are amber.

"We're leaving," I said. "We're going to live in Fur-Rr." (Fur-Rr is what electric dogs call the United States of America.)

"No kidding," Yip said with a shake of his head. "You want to go?"

"I'm not sure," I said. "I guess so. I want to be with my master."

"You trust her?"

"Uh-huh."

**fur** *(Bowwow): yard dog*

**rr** *(Bowwow): land*

“Never trust humans, I say,” Yip said. “No deeper than you can bite them, if you know what I mean.”

“I wouldn’t say that,” I said.

“No?” he said. “See this?” He indicated a welt across his rump. “This is the price of trust.”

“What happened?”

“Group of boys,” he said with a sneer. “With switches. Kept calling me. Whistling. Pretending to have food. Cupping their hands, you know what I mean?”

I did.

“Well, this is nothing new to me,” Yip continued. “I’ve been around the block. But I’m no different than anybody else. I need strokes. So I walk on over, head down, really submissive, no trouble from me. Then *thwack*! And again! And again!” He shuddered.

“How terrible,” I said and gave his wound a lick — at this point, a purely symbolic gesture, I knew.

“Yeah,” he said solemnly. “Still, it’s better being loose. At least out on the street you know what's what. You're a dog, not a pet. You choose your friends. You decide when and where you want to go. It's dangerous, I know. But you're free."

I mulled this over.

"You hear about Hurgh?" Yip asked, his brow furrowing deeper than usual.

"No," I said. "What is it? Parvo?"

"Yup," said Yip. "But then a taxicab came along and got her first." He shook his head.

"I'm sorry, Yip," I said with a whimper. "I know you two were close. She was your cousin, wasn't she?"

"Yeah, but who isn't?" Yip said. "Don't lose any sleep over it, Grumph old boy. It's all just bones in the yard anyway. Just bones in the yard."

♦ ♦ ♦

By the time I returned to Avenida Pichucalco, the rains had begun and Faith had returned from school. She rubbed my coat with a towel.

"Let me show you what I got," she said, dig-

**El conejito andarín** *(Spanish):* **The Runaway Bunny**

**A Faithita, con cariño, Señora Tiza y la clase 4° nivel.** *(Spanish): To little Faith, with affection, Señora Tiza and the fourth-grade class.*

ging into her glittery purple backpack. (She was going through a purple phase.) She pulled out a picture book, *El conejito andarín*. It was the first book in Spanish Faith had ever been able to read through completely.

"Look what they wrote inside," she said. She opened the cover. "*'A Faithita, con cariño, Señora Tiza y la clase 4° nivel.'* And all the kids signed it."

Her shoulders slumped. I knew how she felt. I'd miss my friends, too.

I pawed a pencil out of her bag and took it in my mouth.

"What is it?" she asked. "You want to write something?"

I nodded, and she pulled out her purple notebook and opened it.

I'm scared, I wrote.

"You are?" she asked, putting her arm around me. "Of what, pupplers?"

Leaving home, I suppose, I wrote. Going someplace new.

"Oh, that," Faith said and smiled a little. "I

know how that feels. Don't worry. I'll be with you."

I sighed. Truth be told, until I'd written it, I hadn't even been aware I was scared at all.

"I'll tell you what," Faith said. "How about I ask Hector to help me find the *Peahen*? She's probably still out there by the river. We can pack her up and ship her to San Francisco with the rest of our stuff."

I squinted at her. I wasn't following.

"Then if you don't like it there," she continued, "I'll bring you back. How's that sound?"

My tail wagged. That sounded fine. Just fine.

# Daphne

♦ ♦ ♦ ♦ ♦ ♦ ♦

# 4

Judging from the way I was tossed about in my kennel, the road from San Cristóbal de las Casas down to the Tuxtla-Gutiérrez airport is a steep and winding one. Neither this nor the fog, however, seemed to deter our taxi driver from careering down it at breakneck speed.

**¡Cuidado!** ***(Spanish): Be careful!***

**cúmbias** ***(Spanish): popular dance songs of Mexico***

*"¡Cuidado!"* Bernice shouted at him. The cabbie only snickered and turned up his *cúmbias.*

"Oh, Mama," Faith said, peering into one of my cage's very small vents. "Does he have to ride in this? It's so small."

I whined pathetically.

"Yes," Bernice said, then yelled, *"¡Cuidado!"* again.

Incredibly, within minutes, despite the music and the yelling and the swerving, Faith fell asleep.

I peeked through the vent and saw her hands gently fluttering. I wondered what she was dreaming.

"I'm worried about her," Bernice whispered to Hector.

"Because of the house?" Hector whispered from the front seat.

"We haven't been back there since Luigi died," Bernice said. "Being there is bound to bring back some painful memories."

I didn't understand what they were talking about, and I wanted to. One thing my mother had often told me was that if I ever wanted something — bark.

*"Ruff!"* I said.

**Ruff!**
***(Bowwow):***
***Hey!***

"Quiet!" Bernice snapped.

"I forget he can understand," Hector said. "Shouldn't we tell him?"

Bernice did not reply, but she must have made some sort of sign because Hector twisted around to face me.

"We're going to live in the house that Bernice and Faith lived in in San Francisco," he said. "They lived there with Faith's father, Luigi." He sighed and glanced at Faith. "Luigi died there," he said.

♦ ♦ ♦

I was let out of my cell momentarily in the parking lot of the airport to stretch and relieve myself. Hector removed a pill from the brown bottle Dr. Zarpas had given him and forced it down my gullet.

"That'll make the plane ride easier," he said.

I didn't have time to think what he could have meant by that before I was repackaged, carried into the airport, and put on a cart with other *equipaje*. I was then wheeled out onto an open paved area to the airplane — a jet. The size of it surprised me. The only planes I had ever seen — besides those in my dreams — were those flying high over San Cristóbal de las Casas, and they had always looked so tiny. I knew they only appeared that way because of the distance, but I had no idea they were as big as this. This seemed as big as the cathedral.

The plane's engines screamed louder than anything I had ever heard, even the *Peahen*. Even Bernice. My nostrils burned from the smell of burning fuel. I recalled how the *Peahen* ran on *manteca*, which smelled divine. I didn't know what the jet ran on, but it was surely not the fat of pigs.

**manteca** *(Spanish): pig fat*

I was tossed into a compartment in the belly of the plane. The sounds of the engines muted slightly, and the smell of the fuel was joined by another, more fragrant aroma. It was the smell of beast. Specifically, dog. And a nice-smelling dog at that.

I peeked out the grate to find my kennel pressed up against another kennel. The grates faced each other. I inhaled. The dog smelled of *laurel*. Probably her shampoo.

**laurel** *(Spanish): bay leaf*

She sat with her legs folded under her and her head held high. Her muzzle was long and tapered, her eyes, bulging and black and vacant in expression. She wore a lemon-yellow knit sweater over her speckled brown-and-white coat, and no wonder: she was skin and bone. Rashly, I imagined her

**Roof**
***(Bowwow): Hi***

**Baroo**
***(Bowwow): Excuse me***

**Aroo cur?**
***(Bowwow): Aren't you an electric dog?***

**Oo cur?**
***(Bowwow): An electric dog?***

**Rowr grull?**
***(Arf): Not an electric dog?***

**Eeroo snap!**
***(Arf): I'm a whippet!***

to be a kindred spirit, a street dog, maybe even electric.

*"Roof,"* I said.

She looked away.

*"Baroo,"* I said more politely.

She snorted.

*"Aroo cur?"* I asked.

This moved her. Her eyelids shut. Her head rotated slowly until it was facing me. Her eyes opened. There was contempt in them.

*"Oo cur?"* she snarled. She snarled in Bowwow, but she had a definite Arf accent. (Arf is the language of the dogs of the United States of America.)

I spied a gold tag dangling from her collar. Etched into it was the word DAPHNE.

*"Rowr grull?"* I said in Arf. (I hoped speaking her language might curry favor with her.)

*"Eeroo snap!"* she said, the final word being an actual snap of the jaws.

At that time, I had never seen nor heard of a whippet. Consequently, I'd never heard the Arf word for it. I just thought she was snapping.

I began to apologize for my presumption, but my tongue suddenly flopped out of my mouth as if it were a *pescado*. My knees buckled.

*"Froo garf,"* Daphne said as I collapsed onto the floor of my cell. I could hear her muffled laughter as I slipped into sedation.

**pescado**
***(Spanish):***
***fish***

**Froo garf**
***(Arf):***
***It's the pill***

# Babbo and Veevy

## 5

I awoke the next day in a taxi. The road we traveled was, again, winding and hilly. The view out the windows was — also as before — obscured by fog. It was as thick as *sopa de chícharo.* According to the identification card clipped to the sun visor, our driver was Epifanía Peligrosa. *Cúmbias* played loudly on the radio. Were we back in San Cristóbal de las Casas?

**sopa de chícharo** *(Spanish): pea soup*

*"¡Cuidado!"* Bernice snapped as a sudden stop sent me crashing into the door of the kennel.

*"Lo siento,"* the driver said with a Mexican accent.

**Lo siento** *(Spanish): I'm sorry*

"You awake, widdle wuppler?" Faith cooed, peering in through the vent. "You sure slept a long time."

I grunted.

"You missed Mexico City," she said. "We slept in a hotel and everything. We're almost home now." She looked out the window. "This is Telegraph Hill."

Soon the cab came to a stop. Faith opened her door and my nostrils filled with the smell of coniferous trees, flowers, and unmistakably, the salt of the sea.

"Follow me, wuddlers," Faith said, unlocking the grate. "The steps are kind of tricky."

My legs did not seem my own. They felt numb and stiff and clumpish. What's more, I could hardly see my paw in front of my face. I stumbled several times as I followed Faith down a long, curving wooden stairway, and, once, fell completely off them — into a bed of fuchsias.

"Oh, Eddie," Faith said. "This is no time to dig up flowers."

I just let the comment pass.

About halfway down the stairs, Faith turned suddenly and walked along a cement path to a doorway. She slipped a key into a lock and turned it, then slid another key into another lock and turned it, then yet another key into yet another lock and turned it. Finally, she twisted the doorknob and pushed the door open.

"Here we are," she said. "Home."

We entered a long, tall hall. I had to tilt my head back to see its ceiling. The walls were hung with wooden faces — people's, animals', and mixtures of the two. One was a jaguar mask. Jaguar masks are *corriente* in San Cristóbal de las Casas.

"Mama collects masks," Faith said. "She sells them in her folk arts shop over in Cow Hollow. Some of them are from Africa." She pointed at the jaguar. "That one's from home."

The house smelled musty. I detected the faint aroma of stale perfume — tea tree oil, naturally enough. I also detected a more acrid scent. An old smell. Animal, I was sure. Mammal, probably. More than that I couldn't say.

Faith led me to her room first — down the hall, third door on the right (there were no doors to the left). It was small and square and taller than it was wide. The mammal smell was stronger.

I was very pleased to see a bookshelf brimming

with books. She also had a pink writing desk, a pink bureau with a mirror attached, a pink *armario*, and a pink pinewood toy chest. (She must have passed through a pink phase.) On her bed, atop a pink bedspread, sat a menagerie of stuffed animals.

I jumped up on the bed and tasted them, one by one. They tasted like Faith. Then I jumped down and poked my nose under the bed, the desk, and the *armario*. I found bird feathers under the toy chest, and from under the bureau I pulled out a small cloth packet with the words PURE CATNIP printed on it. I sniffed it and promptly sneezed. (I looked up catnip later in the encyclopedia, dear reader, and discovered it belongs to the *hierbabuena* family. I am allergic to *hierbabuena*.)

**hierbabuena** *(Spanish): mint; literally, good herb*

Faith normally says "*¡Salud!*" whenever I sneeze. But this time she didn't. I looked up to find her sitting cross-legged on the bed, looking down at the catnip I'd found.

**¡Salud!** *(Spanish): Your health!*

"Valentina Vladimirovna Nikolayeva Tereshkova," she said, half-smiling, half-frowning.

I didn't understand what she'd said, but I

sensed what she felt. I jumped up on the bed beside her and lay my head on her lap.

"I named her after the first girl in space," Faith said. "She was Babbo's cat, really. She used to follow him to his shop and lay around all day on his workbench. Then she followed him home at night. We called her Veevy."

She fell silent and when I looked up she was staring at a photograph on the bureau. It was of a man with black hair and a black mustache. He wore glasses and was holding an airplane.

"She was a bluish cat," Faith said. "Babbo said she was purplish, but she was bluish. She wasn't really blue. She was just a little blue. You had to look at her right to see it. Most people said she was gray." She looked down at me and added, "And her eyes were different colors. One was green, one was brown." She laughed. "She was like an *arco iris*!"

**arco iris** *(Spanish): rainbow*

Then suddenly her smile faded and she began twisting her hair in her fingers. I put my forepaws up in her lap and nuzzled in closer. She set her hand on the back of my neck and rubbed gently.

"She disappeared after Babbo died," she said quietly. She leaned over and rested her head on my shoulder.

I looked back at the bureau and noticed, beside the photograph, a brightly colored tin *conejito* holding a tin carrot in its tin paws. Beside the *conejito* was another toy, also made of tin.

**conejito** *(Spanish): bunny*

It was a rocket ship.

# Double Happiness Elementary

♦ ♦ ♦ ♦ ♦ ♦ ♦ ♦ ♦ ♦ ♦

## 6

**Buenos días** ***(Spanish): Good morning***

**¿Tienes hambre?** ***(Spanish): Are you hungry?; literally, Do you have hunger?***

**bistec** ***(Spanish): beefsteak***

"*Buenos días,* Edison," Hector said cheerfully as I stepped into the kitchen the next morning. He stood at the *estufa,* cooking eggs. I couldn't see them in the pan, but I could most surely smell them. *"¿Tienes hambre?"* he asked.

Yes. Yes, I had hunger. I nodded.

"Well," Hector said. "I went shopping." He rustled around in one of the bags. "How about this?"

He held up a cut of red meat. I couldn't smell what it was. It was wrapped in cellophane. He tore the package open and put the chop on a plate for me. Then I smelled it! It was *bistec*! I had never eaten raw *bistec*! It is not something you can ever scrounge. It is never thrown out. I snatched it in my jaws and gnawed it. I felt rich, savory juices run over my tongue and down my throat. It was a dining experience I'm not likely to ever forget.

"Hector's going to the university this morning," Bernice said to Faith as they entered the room a few minutes later. "I'm going to the shop." She guided Faith to a chair at the table and pressed her down onto it. "You're going to school."

Faith stamped her feet. "Schoo-ool?"

"School," Bernice said.

"But what about Eddie?" Faith said.

"He can just stay here and do whatever it is dogs do," Bernice said. "Sleep. Eat."

"Read," Hector said with a sly grin.

Bernice shot him a glance, then ducked behind her newspaper. The headline facing me read:

RENOWNED ANIMAL BEHAVIORIST
SIGNS BOOKS TODAY.

"Who's going to be my teacher?" Faith asked.

"Ms. Ng," Bernice said from behind her paper.

I asked Faith later for the spelling. It was the

first name I'd ever seen without a vowel. Faith said that it's a Vietnamese name, but that Ms. Ng is Chinese.

"What about Alex Wao?" Faith said quietly. "Will he be there?"

"Who's Alex Wao?" Hector asked.

"A jerk," Faith mumbled.

"I think you'd do well to try a little harder with Alex this time, Faith," Bernice said. "Walk away from him if he bothers you." She lowered her paper. "And under no circumstances is there to be any kicking!"

"Couldn't I bring Eddie?" Faith asked, wincing a bit.

"No," Bernice said. "No, you couldn't. And I don't want you talking about —" She looked at me. At the moment, I was laboring hard to get at a particularly elusive bit of gristle. "I don't want you telling the other children about him," she finished.

Faith harrumphed.

After breakfast, Hector put on a suit and tie, kissed Faith's forehead, Bernice's jaw, scratched me between the ears, and left for the university. Bernice put on a black wool skirt and a gray wool sweater and applied some tea tree oil behind her ears. She also dabbed some on the insides of her wrists.

"Have fun in school, dear," she said to Faith. "Say *Ni hao* to Ms. Ng for me."

**Ni hao** *(Chinese): hello*

She picked out an umbrella from the umbrella stand, shook out the dust, and went out into the morning fog.

Faith finished her eggs and licked her plate clean, then said, "Come on, Eddie."

I scooped up my steakbone and followed her down the hall to the closet. She put on a jacket and her backpack, then dug out my leash and clicked it to my collar.

**¡Vámonos!** *(Spanish): Let's go!*

*"¡Vámonos!"* she said.

I dropped the bone. Hadn't I heard Bernice correctly?

"I know, I know," Faith said, turning the doorknob. *"Lo que ella no save no les daña."*

**Lo que ella no save no les daña** *(Spanish): What she doesn't know won't hurt her*

♦ ♦ ♦

I clung close to my master's heels as we walked through the fog. Scents seeped through the haze, swirling intoxicatingly around my head, disorienting me, confounding me. I detected coffee, garlic, pork, tobacco, incense, car exhaust, plus many scents I'd never smelled before. I smelled no street dogs.

"Here it is," Faith said. "My old school."

We stood in front of a glass door. A sign over the door read DOUBLE HAPPINESS ELEMENTARY SCHOOL.

I'd always made a point of avoiding schools. They tend to attract children, at least half of whom are boys. I wasn't really excited about the prospect of voluntarily entering their den.

"I can't wait for you to meet my friends," Faith said.

Printed on the glass door itself was a notice: NO DOGS ALLOWED EXCEPT THOSE ASSISTING SIGHT-IMPAIRED PERSONS. Above the messages on both the notice and the sign were Chinese translations. Due to my limited exposure to Chinese in San Cristóbal de las Casas, I never really had a chance to learn it, and I was anxious to do so. I studied the characters on the notice carefully, hoping at least to figure out which of them represented "dog."

"Don't worry about that," Faith said, pushing the door open. "Ms. Ng will let you stay."

# The Alexes

♦ ♦ ♦ ♦ ♦ ♦ ♦ ♦ ♦ ♦

# 7

"Here you are!" Ms. Ng said happily when we walked into the room. "We were wondering where you were!"

**Lao Shi** *(Chinese): Teacher (an address of respect)*

"My mother says *Ni hao, Ng Lao Shi*," Faith said as she peeled off her jacket.

"Well, how nice!" Ms. Ng said. "Please tell Bernice hello for me as well."

"I brought my electric dog today," Faith said. "I hope that's all right."

**Roor!** *(Bowwow): Sure!*

Ms. Ng looked down at me and smiled. "Yes, you may stay," she said to me. "But you must be kind to our pets. Okay?"

**bock** *(Bowwow): parrot*

*"Roor!"* I said, then took a reconnoitering sniff. Besides boys and girls and Ms. Ng, I smelled rodent, bird, and fowl. I spotted a *bock* in a cage in

the corner. And a *conejillo de Indias* in a cage on a table. Where was the fowl?

**conejillo de Indias** *(Spanish): guinea pig*

"Hi, Faith!" said a girl with short, straight black hair and round pink cheeks. She smiled and her cheeks became rosy red balls.

"Hi, Alex," Faith said a little shyly. The two of them shuffled their feet.

Was this the Alex she'd had so much trouble not kicking? I thought she'd said he was a boy.

"What's with the mutt?" asked a boy pushing his way past Alex.

"I don't like it when you push, Alexander!" Alex said crossly.

The boy pretended not to hear her. He sauntered up to me and set his arms akimbo. He had a glint of mischief in his eyes.

"I like your words, Alexandra," Ms. Ng said. "Would you like to respond to Alexandra's words, Alexander?"

*"Liu leng gou!"* he said. He bent down close and pretended to pick something out of my fur. "I

**Liu leng gou** *(Chinese): Mutt; electric dog*

don't think it should be at school. It has fleas. And it's mangy."

I growled. At the time, I did not have fleas, and I have never had the mange.

"He is not!" Faith shouted.

"Faith," Ms. Ng said calmly. "Do you like it when Alexander speaks to you that way?"

"I don't like it when you talk to me that way!" Faith said firmly and loudly. I noticed her knuckles were white.

Ms. Ng touched Alexander on the shoulder. "Maybe you'd like to find an activity in another area, Alex," she suggested.

"No, thank you, Ms. Ng," he said. "You know, I don't think it's fleas after all." He pretended to inspect what he pretended to remove from my fur. "I think it's lice!" He scratched his hair. "It is lice! I have lice! Your dog gave me lice!"

"Aaargh!" Faith said, kicking out at him.

"Whoa!" Alexander said, spinning away and grinning. "Her dog has lice, and she's rabid!" Some of the children laughed. "We may have to put you to sleep, Faith!" he added.

See what I mean, dear reader, about boys?

"I hate you!" Faith yelled, and flew at him. He danced away.

"Use your words," Ms. Ng kept saying as she tried to get between them.

Suddenly, amidst all the hubbub, I spied the fowl. It was a duck. An instinct awoke inside me. I knew that I'd promised to be nice and that I really should have been defending Faith rather than annoying ducks but I couldn't help myself. I snarled. The duck quacked. Then, I'm ashamed to say, I charged it. It squawked and fluttered. My leash snapped taut. I felt Faith leave the ground.

"*¡Ay!*" she yelled.

**¡Ay!** ***(Spanish): Oh!***

We snagged Alexander with the leash. He and Faith collided, then crashed to the floor. Faith somehow managed to keep her grip on the lead, so I could go no farther. The chase was over. The duck — Ping, by name — settled into a tub of water and made soft honking noises.

"We need to talk," Ms. Ng said, helping Alexander to his feet. She surprised me by appearing quite unruffled. Her voice was soft and clear, and her movements, slow and gentle. "Let's go to the circle," she said.

♦ ♦ ♦

The first thing Ms. Ng did when she joined us on the circular rug was to ask the kids to introduce themselves to Faith and me, and vice versa. Faith hadn't been to Double Happiness Elementary in a long time and so a lot of the children were new to her. Of course, they were all new to me.

I detected many different accents as the kids told their names and said hello. I was sure Noe was from Oaxaca. Joey, Michael D., and Sophie sounded Italian. Chelsea spoke with a Spanish accent, but not Latin-American Spanish, and not the Spanish of Spain. I think it was the Spanish of the Philippine Islands. Jeffrey, Jenny, Wei Ying, Michael X., and the two Alexes had Chinese accents. Pouen said she spoke Cambodian, Lao, Chinese, and English, and was learning French.

"Now, then," Ms. Ng said, laying her hands in

her lap. "Would anyone like to tell me their plans?"

"I'll be more careful to use my words, Ms. Ng," Faith said, "instead of my hands."

There was a pause. Then Ms. Ng said, "Alexander?"

"Not right now, Ms. Ng," he said.

"Maybe later?" Ms. Ng asked.

"Maybe later," he said.

Ms. Ng turned to Alexandra. "I liked your words, Alex," she said.

Alexandra smiled. "Thank you, Ms. Ng."

Then Ms. Ng addressed Faith. "So, Faith, would you like to tell us about your adventures in Mexico? If you don't want to, of course, that's okay."

"Sure," Faith said. "I built a rocket ship and Eddie and I flew to Bone Island in it."

"Duh!" Alexander blurted.

"It's true!" Faith said.

*"Ow owr!"* I growled.

"Yeah, right," Alexander said, and rolled his eyes.

**Ow owr!**
***(Bowwow): It's true!***

"Faith," Ms. Ng interjected, "do you like it when Alexander talks to you that way?"

"I don't like it when you say 'duh!' to me, Alex," Faith said, then slyly stuck out just the tip of her tongue.

"What did you use for fuel?" Alexander said.

"Pig fat," Faith said and folded her arms.

"Yeah, right!" he laughed. "Get NASA on the phone!"

A few children snickered.

Faith jumped to her feet. "I don't like that, Alex!" she said.

"I like your words, Faith," Ms. Ng said. "Would you sit down, please?"

Faith stood glaring at Alexander for a few moments, then slowly resumed her cross-legged position.

"Thank you," Ms. Ng said. "Faith, do you think you could make a working model of your rocket ship here at school for us?"

"I sure can!" Faith said.

"And Alex, perhaps you'd care to help," Ms. Ng added. "I know that you enjoy model rocketry."

"She doesn't need me," Alexander said with a smirk. "She has Edison, her mangy copilot. With lice."

At this, Faith stood, bisected the circle, and kicked him in the elbow.

# Enchanté

♦ ♦ ♦ ♦ ♦ ♦ ♦ ♦ ♦

# 8

Faith sulked as we walked home that afternoon. She mumbled under her breath. She kicked at anything in her path. Pits. Bones. Dried *chicles.* Every so often she'd say "hate him" in a clear voice. Things had not gone well her first day back at school. Ms. Ng had called her aside many times to talk to her about using her words, but she and Alexander had continued to rub each other's fur the wrong way right up until the final bell.

**chicles** *(Spanish): chewing gum*

The fog had lifted and I was finally able to see San Francisco as well as smell it. Everywhere I looked were signs written in Chinese and English. The streets were lined with people and fresh produce in crates. We passed a restaurant and, in the window, barbecued and hung on hooks, were ducks, their heads still intact. I thought of Ping.

"Hungry?" Faith asked.

I looked up at her. She was smiling. I was glad. I nodded.

"Me, too," she said, and opened the restaurant's door.

Out rushed a heavy, meaty odor. My nose throbbed. My tongue swelled. My eyes watered. I liked this place.

"Wait here," Faith said and closed the door behind her.

I paced back and forth along the sidewalk. I whined. I pulled. I slobbered. I scratched at the glass door: *scritch*, *scritch*, *scritch.* Such a terrible sound, but ofttimes effective.

Finally, Faith reemerged with a small white paper bag. My nose told me there was pork inside it. My nose is rarely wrong. Could it be *carnitas*? I am most definitely a dog who loves *carnitas*!

**carnitas** ***(Spanish): roasted pork nuggets glazed in fat drippings***

Suddenly I lunged for the bag! I leapt up on my master! Truly, I was beside myself!

"Easy!" Faith said, giggling, holding the bag up over her head. *"¡Cálmate!"*

I tried to calm down. Really I did. I made myself climb down off her. This wasn't easy. I had to talk to my paws, to my nose, to my tongue. I had to persuade them that they were behaving badly, that they were going about things the wrong way. I had quite a time in doing so, but finally, I convinced them. I forced myself down onto the sidewalk, into a lying position. It took all my mental strength to bestill my body's incessant wriggling, at which I was almost totally successful. Only my tail refused to obey. Tails are like that.

The self-control paid off, though, when Faith withdrew a small, pink nugget from the bag.

**shumei** *(Chinese): pork dumplings*

"It's *shumei*," she said.

Oh, it was too much! There's only so much a dog can take. I dove at the bag. This time I caught it with my teeth and tore it from her hand. I had ripped it to shreds before it had even hit the ground. I acted like I'd never eaten before, like a crazed, wild animal. Like a mad dog.

"Save a couple for me!" Faith said, laughing.

Oh, *shumei* is good! Very porky, very salty. A little rubbery. That's a good thing. I like to chew.

I didn't exactly save her any.

Faith bought another bagful and I agreed not to rip it apart, contenting myself instead with the dumplings that she'd toss to me from time to time as we walked along. I caught each and every one in midair, even the ones she threw badly.

♦ ♦ ♦

We had just crossed a broad, bustling street near a tall, pointy tower (Faith called it a pyramid) when I caught scent of her again. The scent was distinct, unmistakable, like a pawprint. It was *laurel.*

It was Daphne.

I surged forward so abruptly the leash snapped out of Faith's hand.

"Eddie!" she hollered. *"¡Alta!"*

*"Roo! Roo! Roo!"* I barked as I sprinted down the street, around pedestrians' legs and fireplugs and signposts.

"Ed-die!" Faith yelled from behind me. "Wait! *¡Alta!*"

Finally I spotted Daphne across the street. She

**¡Alta!** *(Spanish): Stop!*

**Roo!** *(Arf): Hey!*

was being walked. I was struck by how she moved. She lifted her wrists up high as she went along, lending her gait the springiness and stateliness of a horse in a parade. The muscles in her limbs and neck rippled. Her black ears lay back flat on top of her head, their tips touching. They were folded up elegantly, like bat wings at rest.

I barked again. She did not acknowledge me in any way. Her ears did not even prick up. She just continued on along behind her master. Her posture was impeccable.

Several lanes of cars and buses streamed along between us. I raced up and down the curb, waiting for a lull. The lights changed farther down and I got my chance. Suddenly the street was empty. I bounded across and — cover your eyes, dear reader — I greeted her in a most houndly fashion.

**Fichez le camp!** *(French): Beat it!*

"Oh!" Daphne's master gasped. "*Fichez le camp!* Shoo! Shoo! Stop that!"

Daphne skipped the verbiage. She just bit. My rump. Hard.

**Yowr-rr-rr!** *(Bowwow): Yee-ouch!*

"*Yowr-rr-rr!*" I howled.

"What happened, widdle wuppler?" Faith

cooed, arriving on the scene. She knelt beside me and rubbed my shoulder. (Her intentions were true. Her diagnosis was just off.)

"Your dog is very rude, Mademoiselle," Daphne's master said with a French accent. "You should keep him in a muzzle."

"I'm really sorry," Faith said. "He got away from me."

"He certainly did!" the woman said. "And he *had* his way with my poor Daphne!"

"What a skinny dog!" Faith said. "Is she sick?"

"She's a whippet," the woman said with a sniff. "A purebred. Pedigreed. And she is in *top* condition." She turned up her snout. Daphne did, too.

"This is Eddie," Faith said. "He's electric. I'm Faith." She extended her hand.

Daphne's master took it as if it were a dead bird. *"Enchanté,"* she said. "I am Madame Toutou Moucher. You should call me Madame." She placed the accent on the second syllable: Ma-DOM.

**Enchanté** ***(French): Enchanted; pleased to meet you***

"Yes, Madame," Faith said, with the appropriate stress.

"This is Daphne," Madame said.

"Hello, poochler," Faith said to Daphne.

Daphne curled her fishhook tail inward between her hind legs, and turned away.

"Do you live near here?" Faith asked Madame Moucher.

"Yes," Madame said, with a cough. She was clearly growing weary of chatting with us. "We have a place along the Filbert steps."

"So do we!" Faith chirped. "We're neighbors!"

"Really?" Madame said, looking Faith and me up and down. She shrugged. "How amusing."

"Maybe Eddie and Daphne could play together sometime," Faith suggested. "Eddie doesn't have any friends in San Francisco. Except me, I mean." She smiled.

Madame snorted. Daphne snorted, too.

"I don't think that that would be such a good idea," Madame said. "Daphne is, well, rather *engaged* these days. She's in competition, you know."

"Oh," Faith said, confused. "Sure. I see."

"Yes, well, then," Madame said, turning to leave. "*Adieu. Venez ici,* Daphne."

Daphne followed behind, her nose pressed close into the back of Madame's knee, her ears refolded, winglike, atop her head. She eased back into her horse's prance, her wrists high, her step light.

And I felt, for a moment, that I did not exist.

**Adieu** ***(French): Good-bye***

**Venez ici** ***(French): Come here***

# Harry Swift, Cabaret Singer

♦ ♦ ♦ ♦ ♦ ♦ ♦ ♦ ♦ ♦ ♦ ♦ ♦ ♦

## 9

"This is Babbo's old shop," Faith said.

We stood under a striped canvas canopy in front of a small store front. It was a *zapatería.* A man with white hair was inside soling a shoe.

**zapatería** *(Spanish): shoe store*

"It used to be his fix-it shop," Faith said. "He used to fix toasters and blenders and stuff. He could fix anything."

She leaned forward and pressed her nose against the glass.

"He was an inventor, too," she said. "Like his father. My *nonno* was one of the inventors of the electric rolling pin."

**nonno** *(Italian): grandfather*

I was listening to Faith, dear reader. Honest. But I must admit that, quite out of my control, my attention was being drawn away from her to the shop next door, where, through the large front window, I saw stacks and stacks of books. Taped to the shop's window, a banner read:

AUTHOR SIGNING TODAY, 3:00–8:00 P.M.
HARRY SWIFT, PH.D., WORLD-RENOWNED
ANIMAL BEHAVIORIST AND
AUTHOR OF *WHY DO YOU THINK*
*THEY CALL THEM DOGS?*:
*THE MYTH OF CANINE CONSCIOUSNESS*

"What is it, puppler?" Faith asked. She grinned when she read the banner. "Oh, I see!" She checked her wristwatch. "Okay, let's go in. But we can't stay long. We have to get home before Mama does."

On the door I noticed another of those NO DOGS ALLOWED signs.

"Don't pay any attention to that," Faith said. "It's Dante's shop. She's my friend."

Faith led me into a large room filled entirely with books. They were everywhere you looked! I felt like a kid in a *dulcería* (or a pooch in a *carnicería*).

**dulcería**
***(Spanish): candy shop***

**carnicería**
***(Spanish): butcher shop***

"Can I help you with something?" a woman asked us. Her ink-black hair was tied up in a bun, revealing dark freckles up to her hairline. Her eyes were dark, too, and shimmery. Her English had a slight Italian accent.

**bella somma**
***(Italian):***
***pretty penny***

"Dante! It's me!" Faith said, on her tiptoes.

"Faith!" Dante said happily. "Look at you! Oh, I wish Luigi, your papa — may he rest in peace — could see you! You're a *bella somma*!"

**Grazie**
***(Italian):***
***Thank you***

*"Grazie,"* Faith said.

"Ah, and you speak *italiano*!" Dante said, beaming.

**italiano**
***(Italian):***
***Italian***

"Just a few words," Faith said. "I know *grazie* and *ciao*, and *cannoli*, too."

**ciao**
***(Italian):***
***good-bye***

Dante laughed. "Cannoli! Ha ha! That's very important!" Then she leaned over and kissed Faith's cheek.

"And who's this?" she asked, looking at me.

**cannoli**
***(Italian):***
***a pastry filled with cream and ricotta cheese***

"This is my dog, Edison," Faith said. "He's electric."

"So he is," Dante said, winking at me. "Faith has always been one of my best customers," she told me. "She and Luigi used to come in every day." She turned to Faith. "What happened to your little pussycat? The little purplish one?"

"She was bluish," Faith said. "She ran away after Babbo died."

"Oh, I'm so sorry," Dante said and stroked Faith's orange hair.

"That's okay," Faith said, looking down.

"I heard Bernice remarried," Dante said gently.

"Uh-huh," Faith said, lifting her gaze. "She married Hector."

"Is he nice?"

"Yes, he's very nice," Faith said with a smile.

"I'm glad," Dante said, smiling, too.

"We came in for the book signing," Faith said. "Eddie's very interested."

I wagged my tail.

"I'm sure he is!" Dante laughed. "We'll be starting in a few minutes."

"Come on, Eddie," Faith said. "Let's look at books."

On our way to the children's books, we passed a large sign with the word PETS on it. Smaller signs read CATS, BIRDS, DOGS, REPTILES, FISH, and POT-

BELLIED PIGS. I scanned the shelves in the DOGS section and came upon one succinctly entitled *The Dog Book.* I pulled it down and flipped to the index. Whippets, page 243. On page 243 I saw an animal similar to Daphne. It was not Daphne, of course. There is only one of her.

Whippets, the book said, like greyhounds, descended from the desert dogs of Egyptian pharaohs and Arabian sheiks. Whippets are sight hounds. Sight hounds, as you can probably deduce, have exceptional eyesight, and, unlike most dogs, myself included, rely on it as heavily as they do their sense of smell. Whippets, the book went on, are also quite fleet. Some have been clocked doing in excess of forty miles per hour. Whippets were bred primarily for hunting game — rabbits in particular. In recent years, though, as the popularity of coursing has waned, whippets have been kept mostly as racing dogs, as show dogs, and as pets. The book added that whippets usually have sweet dispositions, though they may seem aloof, even coolly dispassionate. It also said that whippets rarely bark. The author did not know Daphne.

I flipped back to the index. I ran my nail down the E's: ears, eczema, elkhounds. No electric dogs.

"Hello, everybody, and thank you for coming," Dante announced from across the room. She stood behind a table covered with stacks of books. Beside her, a man in a tweed jacket and a green baseball cap smiled and waved a pen. When the people in the store gathered around, she said, "I'm very pleased to introduce to you, Dr. Harry Swift!"

The crowd applauded. The signing had begun.

"Thank you so much," I heard Harry Swift say to someone. "I'm glad you enjoyed it. Who shall I make it to? Is that one L or two?"

"Are you, like, really sure dogs don't think?" asked a man with purplish hair and a gold ring through his eyebrow. "I have a poodle who I think is, like, totally intelligent."

"Dumb as dogwood, all of them," Harry Swift said. "Poodles especially. Next!"

I growled.

"Hark!" Harry Swift said and cupped his ear.

**Canis familiaris** *(Latin): domesticated dog*

"Do I hear the complex language of *Canis familiaris,* the common domesticated dog? Beast of infinite wit and sagacity? Speak, hound, and regale us with your wisdom!" He let out a deep, rippling chortle.

I growled louder.

"Ah, behold the beast!" Swift said, pointing in my direction. The crowd turned. "There is our esteemed companion! Man's best friend! Champion of the hunt! Leader of the pack! Courageous protector of home and hearth! So clever! So true! So obsequious!"

I didn't know what that word meant but I knew it wasn't nice.

**Yur-ark!** *(Bowwow): Egotist!*

*"Yur-ark!"* I barked.

"He speaks!" Swift squealed. "Note the enunciation! The diction! The elocution! Such eloquence! Such pith! This is certainly no lowly creature! No carrier of pestilence and disease! This is not the horrid rabid cur that nips postal carriers nor devours defenseless infants in their cribs! This is no fleabag! No gnawer of expensive leather footwear! This is Dog! The result of centuries of inbreeding! The animal man created to walk with him through this life — especially on cold, drizzly nights. Speak again, magnificent pooch! Speak, mutt, speak!"

*"Roo-ah bowwow ar ur bark!"* I barked.

*"Bravissimo!"* Swift cheered. He stood and slapped his hands together. "Extraordinary! Words cannot do you justice, sir! Clearly I have been misguided! I admit it! Truly you are a creature of superior intelligence! I yield, sir! Humbly, I yield!" And he bowed.

Uneasy laughter rose from the crowd.

Faith led me up to the table.

"Ah! The noble creature's proud keeper!" Swift said. "Would you like me to sign a copy of my book for you?"

"No," Faith said. "I just have a question."

"Shoot," Swift said.

"Let's say you really are wrong," Faith said, "and dogs really *do* think, and maybe even read and write."

"And pigs fly," Swift added, smirking.

"What would you do then?" Faith asked.

**Roo-ah bowwow ar ur bark!** *(Bowwow): You're really barking up the wrong tree!*

**Bravissimo!** *(Italian): Excellent!; Bravo!*

"Well," Swift said, "I used to be a cabaret singer. I was quite good, actually." Then he rocked with laughter.

"That's good," Faith said, not missing a beat. "At least you'll have something to fall back on."

# The Discovery of Electricity

♦ ♦ ♦ ♦ ♦ ♦ ♦ ♦ ♦

# 10

Both Bernice and Hector were home when we finally got there. They met us in the hall.

"Your teacher phoned me at work," Bernice said. Her face was as red as a *belabete*, her eyes, large as eggs.

**belabete** *(Spanish): beet*

"She did?" Faith said as if she couldn't imagine why.

"She said you were having trouble using your words today," Bernice continued. "And that you brought your electric dog to school."

Faith gulped.

"Do you not remember me telling you not to bring Edison to school?" Bernice demanded. "Do you have any idea what would happen if people found out about —" She shot me a glance. "About *him*?"

"Yes, Mama," Faith mumbled.

"Pandemonium!" Bernice shrieked. "Sheer and utter!"

Hector put his hand on Bernice's shoulder. *"Cálmate, mi cielo,"* he said. *"Cálmate."*

**Cálmate, mi cielo** *(Spanish): Calm down, my sky,* or *heaven (a term of endearment)*

Bernice took a deep breath and pinched the bridge of her nose with thumb and forefinger.

"She had a very trying day," Hector whispered to us.

"The dog doesn't go to school," Bernice said with a sigh.

And for the next few days, I didn't. Each morning, after breakfast, Hector would go off to the university and Bernice would walk Faith to school. Then she proceeded on to her folk arts shop. I remained at home. Alone.

I spent the days reading, writing, sleeping, and eating — kibbles mostly. It's awfully hard to go back to dry dog food after you've tasted *bistec* and *shumei*, let me tell you. In the afternoon, when Faith came home, I would listen to her tell me how the model rocket (the *Peachick*, she named it) was coming along, how jerky Alexander was, and how she couldn't wait to see his face when the *Peachick* blasted off.

Through all this, there was one thing that kept creeping into my thoughts, one bone that I couldn't seem to stop gnawing: it was Daphne. This baffled me. Of all the things that could be occupying my mind, why was it she? She had been nothing to me but high-nosed, sniffy, and supercilious. (These are words I found in Faith's thesaurus, under "snooty.")

Then, on the third day of my solitude, a ruckus arose at the front door. I stepped into the hall and saw Hector there, directing a group of men carrying boxes.

"You can just put them in there," he said, pointing to the *sala*. "The big crate goes in the backyard."

The men set their boxes down in the sala, then went back outside. I rushed to one of the boxes and began sniffing and clawing at it. I smelled Faith's clothes inside, and her books — and my bones! Faith had packed my bones! Such a thoughtful girl! I tore through the cardboard and plucked one of them out. Then I ran with it out to the tiny backyard and buried it. Suddenly, somehow, the house seemed much more like my home.

Later, as I lay napping contentedly in a bed of golden poppies, two of the movers came through the back gate carrying a huge, wooden crate. The word *FRÁGIL* was painted in big letters on each side. They set it down beside me with a thunk. When I sniffed faint traces of pig fat coming from the crate, I knew what was inside. Hector had boxed up the rocket and shipped it, just as Faith had asked.

**frágil** *(Spanish): fragile*

That afternoon Faith burst through the back door.

"The *Peahen*!" she cheered, and began dancing around the crate.

Hector appeared at the door with a toolbox. *"Aquí,"* he said to her, holding out a crowbar.

**aquí** *(Spanish): here*

Faith snatched it and began tearing the crate apart. Hector helped with a hammer. Boards and wood shavings flew until, at last, the cargo was revealed.

"We'll show that Alex, won't we, girl?" Faith said to her ship.

The *Peahen*, of course, had seen better days. Her column had been badly dented, her fins bent, her window cracked. Her hatch hung on twisted hinges.

"No sweat," Faith said as if reading my mind. "A little banging here, a little banging there, and she'll be as good as new."

I believed her implicitly, dear reader. I've learned to always believe in Faith's schemes, no matter how wild they may sound. The *Peahen* would fly again. My only wonder was to where.

Hector came out again later with two dishes — pasta with Italian sausage for Faith, just the sausage for me. He also had thoughtfully brought out a pad and pencil for me, should I wish to express myself.

**¡Gracias!** *(Spanish): Thank you!*

¡Gracias! I wrote.

*"De nada,"* Hector said. "It's getting dark, *mi hija*," he said to Faith. "Think about quitting soon."

**De nada** *(Spanish): You're welcome*

"Just a little longer," Faith said and slurped a strand of spaghettini.

"Okay," Hector said. "Just a little longer." He mussed Faith's hair. "Your mama should be home soon," he said. "She called and said she'd be late."

He gave my crown a rub, too, then went back inside. The porch light came on.

We sat silently awhile, chewing. Then I wrote, Why did Harry Swift call the dog "the animal man created"?

Faith thought a bit, then said: "Some people think that human beings tamed wild dogs."

Like wolves? I wrote. I had never seen or smelled a wolf, but I had read "Little Red Riding Hood" and "The Three Little Pigs."

"Wolves, foxes, hyenas, jackals, coyotes," Faith said. She took her last bite and wiped her dish clean with her bread. "I read about it once in the encyclopedia. It said that we took the runts of wild dog litters and bred them together."

Why? I wrote.

"To make dogs that act like puppies," she explained. "Then they would be tamer and we could keep them. For hunting." She smiled. "Or for pets."

I thought of the roaming street dogs of San Cristóbal de las Casas. They were neither pets nor hunters, unless you consider scavenging for food hunting. Why were *they* made?

Do you believe it? I wrote.

"I don't know," Faith said. "Maybe dogs just tamed themselves."

Why would they do that?

"Because they liked being around people, I guess," Faith said, and she smiled again.

I thought for a minute, then wrote, Then all dogs descended from wild dogs?

"Yep," Faith said.

So all dogs are crossbreeds? Mutts?

"I guess so," she said, thinking.

So then we're all electric?

Faith laughed. "I guess you're right! I never thought of that! I guess that means even poodles came from wild dogs! Ha!"

And what about you? I wrote.

"What do you mean?" Faith asked. She stabbed a sausage link and fed it into her mouth.

Your father was Italian. What's Bernice?

"Scottish-Irish-German," Faith said with her mouth full. Suddenly she brightened. "She's electric!" she said. Then she frowned, fiddled with her lip, and squealed, "*I'm* electric!"

I slurped her happy face. I love marinara sauce.

We licked our dishes clean and then Faith wiped her face with her sleeve.

Would you let me out for a while? I wrote.

"Why?"

I want to find that dog, I wrote. The skinny one. Daphne.

"Do you know where she lives?"

I can find her.

"How?"

I sniffed exaggeratedly.

"Oh," she said. "Can't I come with you?"

I need to go alone.

She paused, then said, "Okay. But don't be gone long. And stay away from the streets. Dogs aren't supposed to run loose in San Francisco.

That Madame woman said they live around here. On the steps."

I remember, I wrote. I'll find her.

"Okay," Faith said again, and opened the back gate for me. *"Cuidado,"* she whispered.

I ran out into a small grassy ravine and began to sniff the air for the whippet. From behind me came the reverberating sound of a rubber hammer pounding a tin rocket ship.

# Bernice's Undoing

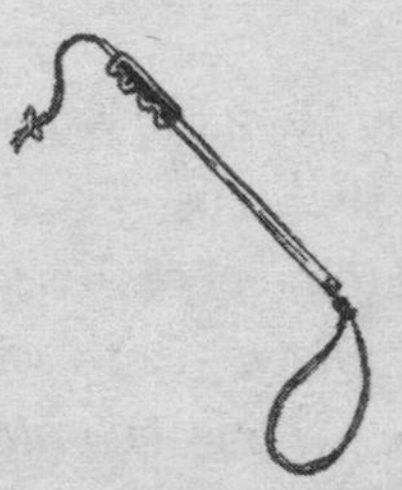

# 11

My first whiff of Daphne came wafting down from above, down through the branches of the coniferous trees. I wondered if whippets roosted.

The scent led me around to the back of a tall, wood-shingled house. There was a porch at ground level with a terrace above it. The scent came from the terrace. I heard the tinkling of dog tags, and a light sniff, and knew I'd come to the right place.

*"Roo!"* I said as softly as I could.

Daphne's head poked out through the balustrade.

**Ba-ba-ra!**
***(Arf): Intruder!***

*"Ba-ba-ra!"* she barked. *"Ba-ba-ra!"*

**Loor!**
***(Arf): Please!***

*"Loor!"* I whined.

*"Ba-ba-ra! Ba-ba-ra!"* She began hopping up and down.

*"Raboo, loor!"* I begged.

Her barrage only intensified. I could not get a word in edgewise. I could not hear myself think.

"Daphne!" a voice cried from the terrace. Madame's face appeared over the rail. "Oh!" she said when she saw me. "It's you, *sale chien! Fichez le camp! Fichez le camp!*"

I looked at the two of them, snapping and barking and starting to foam at the mouth, and decided it would probably be best to just go home, regroup, and think about my next move. I didn't even attempt good-bye. I just turned tail, and slunk away.

Before I'd gone far, I encountered a man walking toward me wearing white gloves and carrying a long silver pole, which had a loop dangling from its end. He held it with both hands, horizontally across his body.

"That's a good dog," he said comfortingly. "That's right. You're a *good* dog."

I approached him, my head down. After the shellacking Daphne and Madame had just given me, I was in need of a little unconditional positive

**Raboo, loor!** *(Arf): Excuse me, please!*

**sale chien!** *(French): dirty dog*

regard. I wagged my tail as a sign that I wanted what he was offering.

You see, I couldn't have known what he was offering.

That's when I discovered the use of the come-along — the thing he was carrying. The loop was a rope noose, which he deftly slipped over my head. Then, quick as a hare, he pulled a knot at the other end of the pole and the noose tightened around my neck.

"That's a good dog," he said. "I'm not going to hurt you."

I tried to bark but the rope constricted my throat. I couldn't make a sound. I flailed and clawed to no avail.

He walked me down the steps to the street, where a van was parked, its rear doors open. On the side it read SAN FRANCISCO ANIMAL CARE AND CONTROL. I was put in the van, into a cage, and the van's doors were slammed shut.

Then I was taken downtown, and booked.

♦ ♦ ♦

Never had I been in a place with such a high concentration of canines in such close quarters. I nearly swooned from the smell. Suddenly I knew where San Francisco's street dogs were. They were in jail.

I was put into a kennel quite different from my own. It was a wire box. I was not read my rights nor told why I was being held.

In the cell adjacent to mine was a short-legged, pointy-faced, black-and-white dog with FRANKLIN etched on his tags. He wore a flea collar, poor pooch — nasty-smelling things, flea collars — and kept insisting that his master would be in to pick him up very soon.

"This is his golf day," he told me in Arf. "He's probably on the links now. Tenth, eleventh hole, I'd say, depending on his game. Usually goes to the clubhouse afterward. He'll be down after he gets home and picks up his messages. They call if you have tags, you know. He'll curse himself for not mending that fence. Should be here very soon. I'm just glad I have tags."

I had tags, dear reader, but not San Francisco tags. Mine were San Cristóbal de las Casas tags:

EDISON, EL PERRO CORRIENTE
REG. #00000053
11 AV. PICHUCALCO, S. C. L. C.
967-08438

How was Faith going to find me?

On my opposite side was a brown dog with gnarled ears. Her brow was furrowed. She smelled of garbage. Street dog, I thought. She didn't respond when I spoke to her. The only sounds I heard from her were sighs, slow and deep and labored. I decided to just let the sleeping dog lie.

Directly across the aisle was a dog with stiff, gray fur, and a black spot covering her left eye. Some kind of shepherd, I think. She was too far away for me to read her tag.

"My name is Grumph," I said to her.

"I'm Yark," she replied. "You're not from here, are you?"

"No," I said. "I'm from Mexico. Is my Arf that bad?"

"No," she said, "but you do have an accent."

"How long have you been in here?"

"A day or so," she said. "My master's on vacation. A friend of hers goes by the house to look in on me. Supposed to do it every day. Sometimes he neglects to. That's how I ended up here. I was hungry and got out of the yard. Then they nabbed me."

"That rope thing?"

"Yeah, the come-along," she said. "How'd they get you?"

"I'd slipped out to see a whippet," I said with a snap.

One of the screws (that's inmate slang for guards) entered the ward later with a woman. The animals whined in unison.

"There he is!" the woman squealed, indicating a silly-looking terrier with a white woolen coat. He looked like a sheep.

"Oooh, pookums!" the woman said. "Come to mumsy!" Apparently, she knew Widdlish.

"You'll need to come back to the desk," the screw said. "There are some citations to take care of."

"Citations?" she said. "You mean *fines*? I have to *pay* to get my puppy back?"

"Yes, ma'am."

"Why, that's dognapping! You're holding my pookums for ransom!"

"I'm sorry, ma'am, but we have costs. And there are city ordinances. Your dog was at large."

"At large, indeed!" the woman said. "This is an outrage!" And she stormed out of the room.

The screw shrugged and followed after her.

"There'll be some hell to pay there," Yark said.

The sheep-terrier paced nervously in his cage.

"Not for me there won't be," Franklin said. "The master's a good egg. I'm sure he'll find humor in this."

For the first time, I wondered how Bernice might react.

A few hours later, a screw led another woman through the ward.

"What happens to the dogs that aren't picked up?" the woman asked as she scanned the pens.

"After four days here, we send them to adoptive services," the screw said.

"Do they put them to sleep?" the woman asked.

"Only in certain cases. Say, for example, the animal's in poor health, or displays unsafe behavior, or is very old. In those cases we might euthanize."

"You mean, put them to sleep?" the woman asked. "*Kill* them?"

"We prefer 'euthanize,'" the screw said.

Fortunately, I did not fall into one of those three dreadful categories. I looked at the brooding, shaggy mutt beside me. Was she sick? How old was she? She never barked — did she bite?

"The cats are over here," the screw said.

The woman found her precious pet — a large, muscular, orange tom who rubbed his body against the cage when his master appeared.

*"Yowr-rew,"* he said.

**Yowr-rew** *(Mew): About time*

I never had much contact with cats in San Cristóbal de las Casas. It was definitely a dog town. Still, I did encounter one from time to time, often enough to pick up some of their languages. Obviously, I could no more speak a feline tongue (be it Miau, the most common language of Mexican cats, or Mew, the tongue of most of the cats I've encountered from the U.S.A., or Yiaow, that peculiar patois of the Siamese cat) than I could a human one. I am just not equipped for it. But, within limits, I do understand them. I have never, alas, met one who could understand me. Consequently, we have never been able to communicate. This has kept us at a distance.

The tom's master and the screw departed to complete the necessary paperwork just as a man was ushered in wearing green-and-purple checked slacks and a pink short-sleeved shirt. He looked like an *arco iris.*

"Frank!" he exclaimed.

Franklin cowered in his cage.

"You ungrateful cur!" the man yelled. "I ought to just leave you here!"

"Come this way, sir," the screw said. "I need you to fill out some forms, and there's the small matter of the citations."

"Citations!" the man shrieked. "Frank, just you wait until I get you home!" And he left, huffing and puffing. His scent lingered: gin.

"He really is a nice fellow," Franklin stammered. "Really he is. He tipples sometimes is all. Nice fellow."

And then, through the door, came Faith!

"Oh, Eddie!" she cried, rushing up to my cell. "Are you all right? I never should have let you out!"

*"Grumph groo,"* I answered.

**Grumph groo** ***(Bowwow): I'm fine***

"I'm so glad," Faith said with a sigh.

It was almost as if she understood me.

"I called every shelter in town looking for you," Faith said. "Then the man here said they'd picked up a dog with amber eyes and a worried look, so we came right down."

I hadn't noticed at first, but Bernice and Hector were there as well. Hector was smiling. Bernice was not.

"Please come with me," the screw accompanying them said.

"You'll be free soon," Faith said to me as she and Bernice and Hector followed the screw to the door.

"Citations!" I heard Bernice shriek.

After they had gone, I looked over at the sleeping dog beside me. "What'll happen to her?" I asked Yark.

**Bu Grumph**
*(Bowwow): My name is Grumph*

"Adoptive services, I suspect," Yark said. "Hasn't said a word since I got here."

"Maybe I can help," I said to the sleeping dog in Arf. "I'll check up on you from the outside."

**Roo-ah Cur-Rr!**
*(Bowwow): You're Mexican!*

She made no sign of hearing.

"My name is Grumph," I said. "I can help."

Still nothing.

*"Bu Grumph,"* I said in Bowwow. It was worth a shot.

**Aroo bu?**
*(Bowwow): What's your name?*

Her ears pricked up!

*"Roo-ah Cur-Rr!"* I said.

She sat up. Her eyes were amber-colored.

*"Aroo bu?"* I asked.

**Grumph garfroo**
*(Bowwow): I'll check on you*

"Murl," she said.

Yark looked up. "She spoke!" she said.

The screw came back then and unlocked my cage.

*"Grumph garfroo,"* I said to Murl.

**Urf**
*(Bowwow): Thanks*

*"Urf,"* she said.

The screw attached a lead to my collar and led

me out of the cage. I noted the case number on the front of Murl's pen: #414-0-7734.

"Good-bye, Grumph," Yark said. "Good luck with your whippet."

"Thanks," I said. "Good luck with your house sitter." As I passed her pen, I checked her case number, too, for good measure. #414-0-7722.

In the car, I wrote a note to Faith about Murl and Yark and asked if she would check up on them, and she said of course she would. Then she attached my new San Francisco tags to my collar and patted my side.

"There," she said. "Now you're street legal!"

"That dog," Bernice sighed, "will be my undoing."

# Till Prepar'd for Longer Flight

♦ ♦ ♦ ♦ ♦ ♦ ♦ ♦ ♦ ♦ ♦ ♦ ♦ ♦

# 12

The next morning, after Bernice and Faith had left for Double Happiness Elementary, Hector went to his room and began packing a suitcase. I fetched my writing gear and stood in his doorway, awaiting an invitation to enter.

"Something on your mind?" he asked.

I jumped up on the bed. Where are you going? I wrote on my pad.

"To Los Angeles," he said. "For a conference."

The Angels? I wrote.

"*¡Sí!*" he said. "*Los angeles.* I'm going to the Angels. It's a city."

Is it in Mexico? I wrote.

"No, it's in California," Hector said, putting folded briefs in his case. "Many places in California have Spanish names. Like San Francisco."

**¡Sí!** *(Spanish): Yes!*

**Los angeles** *(Spanish): The angels*

Saint Francis, I wrote.

"That's right," he said. "Even California is a Spanish name. That's because California used to be a part of Mexico."

I didn't know that, I wrote.

*"Sí, es verdad."*

He rolled up a leather belt, put it in the suitcase, then snapped the case shut.

How long will you be gone? I wrote.

"Just until tomorrow," he said. "Will you look after Bernice and Faith?"

*Sí, claro*, I wrote. *No te preocupes.*

*"¡Gracias!"* Hector said.

Hector, I wrote. May I ask your advice?

"Sure." He sat down beside me. "A little talk, huh? Man to dog."

I met this *perra*, I wrote. She won't give me the time of day.

*"Veo, veo,"* he said, nodding.

She's pedigreed, I wrote. Purebred. And I'm electric.

"We're all electric," Hector said.

That's what Faith said, I wrote.

**es verdad** *(Spanish): it's true*

**Sí, claro. No te preocupes** *(Spanish): Yes, sure. Don't worry*

**perra** *(Spanish): female dog*

**Veo, veo** *(Spanish): I see, I see*

"Why don't you show her you can write?" Hector suggested.

But I don't know if she can read.

Hector laughed. "So read it to her," he said. "Recite for her a love poem."

I've never written poetry before, I wrote.

"Just a second," Hector said. He went to his bookshelf and selected a book.

"Take a look at this," Hector said, laying the book beside me. *An Annotated Treasury of Love Poetry,* it was called. "You'll soon get the hang of it."

I flipped the book open and read:

> O, that you were yourself, but, love, you are
> No longer yours than you yourself here live

I looked at Hector with what must have been a rather baffled expression.

"It's Shakespeare," he said with a grin. "Here. Let's start with something simpler."

He flipped to the table of contents, then to another poem, this one by W. H. Auden.

"Try this one," Hector said.

It was entitled "The More Loving One."

Looking up at the stars, I know quite well
That, for all they care, I can go to hell,
But on earth indifference is the least
We have to dread from man or beast.

I understood it! What's more, I liked it! My tail pounded on the bed.

"You got it," Hector said and patted my shoulder. *"Buena suerte."*

**Buena suerte** *(Spanish): Good luck*

Then he scooped up his gear and left for the Angels.

◆ ◆ ◆

There is a peculiar agony that comes when one wants to write but cannot summon the words. For me, it is marked by a twanging sound in the head, as if someone is stretching my brain to its full extent and then strumming it, as one would an *harpa*. Perhaps, dear reader, you experience it dif-

**harpa** *(Spanish): harp*

ferently. Perhaps, if you're one of the lucky ones, you never have this trouble at all. All I ask is, as you read this story, please try and remember that each word of it came from my pen, which was moved by my snout, which was directed by my twanging dog brain. And be kind.

The poem did not come easily. I fought with it all day long. I paced the house a hundred times. I read poem after poem after poem from Hector's book. They were mostly elegant and charming and poignant — quite unlike mine.

But then I stumbled across "The Garden," a poem by Andrew Marvell, a 17th-century English poet. The word "Daphne" appears in it, which is, I'm sure, how it caught my eye.

> The gods, that mortal beauty chase,
> Still in a tree did end their race:
> Apollo hunted Daphne so,
> Only that she might laurel grow;[12]

The little twelve printed at the end of the verse led me to the bottom of the page, where I found a list of numbered notes. The twelfth described the myth of Apollo and Daphne. Allow me to relate it to you, dear reader, in case you do not know it:

Daphne was a nymph, a minor river goddess. The god Apollo fell in love with her after Cupid (a boy with wings and a bow) shot him with a special gold-tipped arrow. Cupid, in his mischief, also fired an arrow at Daphne — hers, lead-tipped — provoking the opposite emotion in her: she instantly hated Apollo. (I wondered if maybe Cupid had been practicing his archery on Daphne and me that day on the plane.) When Apollo began reciting words of love to her (luckily for him, he was the god of poetry), Daphne fled in disgust.

"Do not fly me as a lamb flies the wolf, or a dove a hawk," Apollo called after her. "It is for love I pursue you."

Daphne ran faster.

So Apollo hunted her as would a hound a hare. Daphne was swift and nimble, and knew the woods well. But Apollo was swifter and nimbler, and was soon breathing down her neck. In desperation, Daphne called upon her father, the river god, for help. Suddenly she felt a stiffness spreading in her body. Her skin became encased in bark. Leaves sprouted from her fingertips. Her feet sank into the soil and rooted there. She had become a laurel tree!

Even still, Apollo loved her. (This may seem strange — to love a tree — but, as a dog, I can accept it.) He continued to visit her and speak his words of devotion, and, eventually, Daphne, the laurel tree, bowed her head to him, and reciprocated.

The story inspired me. The shape of a poem began to show its contours. Though clearly I was no god of poetry, I did feel a strong kinship toward poor Apollo. I empathized. And I began to feel like a poet.

Then I read these lines further down in the poem:

> My soul into the boughs does glide:
> There, like a bird it sits and sings,
> Then whets and combs its silver wings,
> And, till prepar'd for longer flight,
> Waves in its plumes the various light.

And I had it! I had my image! Wings! Flight! These are recurring themes in my work, dear reader, are they not?

I snatched my pen and sprinted through the first stanza. I felt the rhythm in my bones. The endings rhymed effortlessly, naturally. I executed the second stanza nearly as easily, then sped through the third, longest stanza with barely a hitch. The final verse was as easy as taking candy from a puppy

I read it back. I read it aloud, in Arf, to test its euphony — its pleasure to the ear. It sounded right. It rang true. I tinkered with it a bit — changed a word or two here and there — and then it was ready. I was ready.

On to my nymph!

# The Hound Becomes the Hare

# 13

I went into the bathroom and checked my look in the mirror. Passable. I licked my paw and patted down a cowlick on my crown. It popped back up. I checked my teeth and decided I should probably stop and chew something — some rawhide maybe — before heading out. I held a paw up and noticed it was trembling.

When I stepped out into the hall, Faith burst through the front door.

"Eddie!" she squealed. "The *Peachick* flew!" She tossed her backpack aside and tugged off her jacket. "You should've seen Alex's face!"

I ran to her and licked her ear congratulatorily.

"I need to get the *Peahen* operational again," she said. "Today."

I raised a quizzical eyebrow.

"I invited Alex over tomorrow," she said, "for a launch."

I thought for a moment, then ran into our room for paper and pencil.

"What is it?" Faith called, following behind me.

We met up on the bed.

Can I bring a friend? I wrote.

"A friend?" she asked, surprised. "Who?"

Daphne, I wrote.

"I didn't think she liked you."

She had a point.

I have a plan, I wrote. I've written a poem. I'm going to read it to her.

"Okay, but let me come with you this time," Faith said seriously. "Remember the dogcatcher. I'll be the lookout."

No, I have to go alone, I wrote.

We stared at each other. She gave a mild blast of her nostrils. I blasted mine. She scrunched up her eyebrows. I scrunched up mine. It was a standoff.

Finally, she sighed and I licked her nose.

"This time," she said, "if you see the dog-catcher — run!"

♦ ♦ ♦

Licensed and at large, I crept through the ravine to Daphne's house. I set the poem down on the grass and inhaled. She was up there.

*"Ba-ba-ra!"* she yelled from the terrace. *"Ba-ba-ra!"*

"It's just me!" I said in a feeble voice. "Grumph!"

To my amazement, she ceased the alarm.

"You!" she said. "You have a lot of nerve showing up here again after what happened last time!"

"You saw?" I asked, cringing.

"You're crazy to go out without a tether," she said. "When Madame hears us barking she'll probably call the authorities. She probably already has. She's quite high-strung."

"Then I haven't much time," I said, mustering my courage. "What is your name?"

"Lorl," she said.

Lorl! Pronounced so close to the English "laurel" as to be indistinguishable! Laurel! Spelled the same as the Spanish word for bay leaf — *laurel*! Laurel — the tree Daphne became! Lorl!

"Lorl," I said, masking my excitement. "Would you like to come to my master's house tomorrow afternoon?"

"Why?" Daphne asked suspiciously.

"There's something I'd like you to see," I said.

"No," she said. "I can't just —" She stopped. Squinted. "Dogcatcher!" she barked. "Nine o'clock!"

Sure enough, there stood another animal control officer (I understand they no longer care for "dogcatcher"). She held a come-along in her hands.

"That's a good dog," she said. "I'm not going to hurt you."

Yeah, right. I took to my heels. As I fled, I heard the call of a dove, the sound of a ringing bell — it was Lorl!

*"Groo-oorr!"* she howled.

**Groo-oorr!**
***(Arf): Run!***

The chime of her voice vibrated through me,

electrified me, empowered me with fleetness of paw and sharpness of wit such as I'd never known before. Lorl *cared*, so the animal control officer had her work cut out for her.

I ran down the steps as fast as my four gangly legs would carry me. I could hear my pursuer hot on my tail. At the street, I did a reckless thing — I darted across without checking. I doubted the officer would do the same. Tires squealed and drivers swore. When I reached the other curb, I looked back and saw her weaving between the cars. I was impressed.

"That's a good dog!" she was calling. "That's a good dog!"

I tried every trick in the book. I dodged and ducked and doubled back. I could not shake her. Soon the smell of the sea was stronger than ever. I ran past a sign that read PIER 39 onto a kind of *mercado* — wooden-floored and, fortunately, jammed with people. The scent of my would-be apprehender became lost amid the aromas of the strange foods they sold there. (Faith later identi-

**mercado** *(Spanish): market*

fied for me cotton candy, nachos, and the unfortunately named hot dogs.)

One smell in particular seized my attention. It was rancid and foul — just my cup of tea. I followed my nose into a cluster of people pressed up against a railing, all chattering and pointing out to sea. When I followed their fingers I spotted a wooden raft covered with the oddest-looking creatures I'd ever seen. They were long, dark, plump, and shiny. They had whiskers like a cat and fins like a fish. These creatures ***barked.***

I didn't know the dialect.

I barked back. I barked in Bowwow, in Arf, in Ruff, in Grr — in all the dog languages I knew. Still, their responses remained unintelligible to me.

Finally, a little girl holding what I now know was cotton candy stepped up to the railing and revealed the animals' breed.

"Look, Mommy!" she squealed. "Seals!"

♦ ♦ ♦

I made my way home without incident. I barked at the rear gate and Faith let me in. She gathered me up in her arms and hugged me so tightly I thought she might imbed my new San Francisco dog tags permanently into my throat.

"Oh, I was so worried!" she said at last. "You were gone so long!"

Then she stepped back and looked at me. "So," she said, straightening her skirt. "Did she like the poem?"

The poem! Where was it?

# Bait

# 14

"How will I get her to come?" Faith asked me that night as we sat on the bed.

Call her up, I wrote. Invite her.

"But she's a grown-up," Faith said. "She won't come."

I hadn't thought of that.

"I know!" Faith said suddenly. Then she whispered, "I'll pretend I'm Mama!"

I cocked my head.

"Don't you get it? I'll call and say —" She pretended to lift a phone receiver. "'Hello, Madame Moucher? This is Bernice Urquhart — your neighbor? Yes. I was wondering if you'd care to drop by tomorrow for coffee. Splendid! About three? Perfect! Oh, and bring that lovely dog of yours. Ta-ta!'" She hung up her pretend handset and giggled.

But Bernice won't really be here, I wrote.

"No," Faith whispered. "She's usually at the shop until at least five."

Won't Madame be angry? I wrote.

"Probably," Faith said. "But she'll bring Daphne, and that's what you wanted, isn't it?"

I nodded.

**Bueno** *(Spanish): Good*

*"Bueno,"* Faith said, pleased with herself. "I'll make coffee and tea and I'll pick up some snacks. I'll get you some *shumei.*"

Ah, the Chinese *carnitas*! I drooled.

"I'll get some cannoli, too," Faith continued. "It'll be a real launch party!"

I became so excited I jumped off the bed, ran into the hall, into the *sala,* back into the hall, then back into our room. I jumped up on the bed and licked Faith's face until she fell over.

"Stop!" she cried. "Let me up! Let me call her!"

I pressed my ear up to the receiver when she called so I could hear Madame's answer.

"We'd be delighted," Madame said in a delighted voice. "See you at three. *Adieu.*"

Thank you, I wrote.

"How do you say 'thank you' in Bowwow?" Faith asked.

*"Urf!"* I barked.

"Quiet!" Bernice yelled through the wall.

♦ ♦ ♦

I had the whole next day alone to anticipate the day's upcoming events. I paced. I ate. I napped. I fretted. Would she come? Could I get her aboard? Would she bite?

I got Hector's book of poetry down from the shelf and sat awhile with it on the floor. I flipped to the Shakespeare sonnet that had confounded me before (number XIII) and found that, with some deep concentration and some strenuous bone-gnawing, I could understand it. What's more, it was beautiful. I decided to bring the book along. Before I knew it, the clock had chimed three.

Faith burst through the door laden with bags. (She makes a habit of bursting through doors, dear reader.) My nose told me that inside the bags were *shumei*, *manteca*, and jalapeño peppers. I wondered for a moment where she had gotten the *manteca*, but decided that, in a place with a Spanish name, it must be available somewhere.

"T minus thirty minutes!" Faith announced.

Alexander came in behind her.

"So where's this alleged spacecraft?" he asked, dumping his backpack onto the floor.

"Out back," Faith said. "This way."

I hung back a bit in order to slip Hector's book — and paper and pen — into Faith's backpack. Then I joined them out at the launchpad.

The *Peahen* looked shipshape. Her body showed signs of the hammer, but, all things considered, she had retained her figure well. The small, round window was still cracked, but the hinges on the hatch had been repaired and the fins reshaped. Inside sat the same two red-varnished pine chairs — one for the pilot, the other for the copilot. Who would sit in them?

"What's with the garbage can?" Alex said, kicking the *Peahen*.

"It's not a garbage can!" Faith snapped and whacked him on the arm.

She loaded the pig fat into the fuel tank. The smell broke my heart. Why couldn't her ship run on something less scrumptious? Like kibbles? Or jet fuel? It seemed such a tragic waste of good fat. She sprinkled some minced jalapeño peppers in, then shut the tank's door.

"What — no onions?" Alex quipped.

Another whack on the arm.

The doorbell rang.

*"Lorl ayoo!"* I howled.

**Lorl ayoo!**
***(Bowwow): She's here!***

I ran inside, through the kitchen, into the hall. I smelled perfume — French perfume — and lots of it. Madame, I thought. Had she brought Daphne? If so, where was her scent? I scrambled down the long hall, my claws clicking on the hardwood floor. I squeezed my nose as far as I could under the door and inhaled deeply.

It was there! She had come! The scent was there!

*¡Laurel!*

When Faith finally reached the door I was wriggling and whimpering on the doormat, driven mad by the day's wait and Daphne's musky fragrance.

"Pull yourself together," Faith whispered to me. "Calm down. If you're going to impress her, you have to be cool."

She was right. Absolutely right. I sat up. I closed my eyes. Took a deep breath. Counted to ten.

"You ready now?" Faith asked.

I exhaled slowly through my nose, then nodded.

Faith opened the door. Daphne stood on the front stoop, Madame Toutou Moucher at her side.

"You!" Madame said, sneering. Daphne sneered, too. "I might have known! And that horrible dog, too!"

Meaning me.

"My mother informed me she had invited you for coffee," Faith lied. "She called to say she's running a little late. She asked me to make you comfortable until she arrives. Please come in."

Madame squinted at Faith. She glared at me. "Oh, may as well," she said finally, and pushed past Faith into the house.

She stepped into the *sala*, slipped off her lemon-yellow cardigan, and handed it to Faith. A lemon-yellow, brimless hat sat atop a crop of bristly, auburn hair, cut very short. Her face was gaunt, her limbs long and slender. She and her whippet made a matched set.

"Your hat?" Faith politely asked.

"I'll keep it on, thank you," Madame said. She sat demurely on the edge of the sofa cushion, her hands crossed at the wrists, a small purse clutched in one of them.

Daphne aped her master's every move. She fussed when Madame fussed. She yawned when Madame yawned. She sniffed, and puffed, and snorted, *à la* Madame. She wore her lemon-yellow sweater, too — the one she'd worn on the plane.

"I was about to serve some coffee and cannoli in the yard," Faith said. "May I offer you some?"

**à la** ***(French): in the manner of***

Boy, she was good at this hostess stuff!

I could see Madame's mouth water, but then she patted her flat tummy and said, "Maybe just some coffee. Decaf. No cream."

As the humans socialized, I laid a trail of *shumei* leading along the ground to the rocket's open hatch, then set a large dish of them inside. Daphne eagerly fell into the little trap. She boarded the *Peahen* without even knowing it, and dove into the dumplings. Porklust, it's worth noting, crosses all bloodlines.

I realize now, dear reader, that it wasn't really necessary to trick her. But, at the time, I could not forget how our first encounters had gone. I had tried being cordial, and she had been openly, even demonstrably, hostile. True, the last time I had seen her she had actually deigned to speak to me, and had even warned me of the animal control officer. But now she was behaving as before — snooty, supercilious, high-nosed, sniffy. It was my hope that, up in the rocket, far from earth and things earthbound, away in the sky with the clouds for relief, we could talk, become acquainted. And then she'd see that, electric or otherwise, I was worth knowing.

Anyway, that was the plan.

I rejoined the people as they sat around a small table enjoying a nice pre-launch snack. Madame sipped her decaf and nibbled at just the "teeniest sliver" of cannoli. Alex crammed a whole pastry into his mouth. Faith just watched, smiling, the proper hostess, waiting for her moment to come.

"All right!" Alex said after his third cannoli. "Let's get this show on the road!"

Faith leapt to her feet. "Roger that!" she said.

# The Fifth Rocketeer

♦ ♦ ♦ ♦ ♦ ♦ ♦ ♦ ♦ ♦ ♦ ♦

# 15

Faith situated herself in the red pilot's chair. I crawled beneath it. Alex sat in the copilot seat — my former seat. Daphne, stuffed to the flews with pig meat, lay on the floor under Alex, snoring. Her paws waved in the air.

Frankly, I was surprised that we all fit so comfortably. Dogs don't really take up much room, I guess, especially skinny ones. Even so, I didn't think one more creature could have fit aboard.

I was wrong.

"T minus fifteen seconds," Faith announced after she had completed her systems check. Then to Alex she added, "Better buckle up, crewman."

"Yeah, right," Alex said, smirking.

"Little girl!" Madame called from outside. "Will your mother be much longer? Little girl?"

"Commencing countdown," Faith said, withdrawing a matchstick from its box. "Ten . . . nine . . . eight . . . seven . . . six . . ."

"Four . . . nine . . . thirteen . . . eighty-two . . ." Alex said.

Faith glared at him. "Ignition!" she shouted. She struck the match and touched it to the end of the long fuse. The flame whizzed along toward the fuel tank.

"Brace yourself," Faith said to Alex. "It shakes a lot during blast-off."

"Yeah, right," Alex said again.

Then, above the sound of the fuse fizzling, and Daphne snoring, I heard Madame Moucher again, saying to someone, "Well! At last! *Comment allez-vous, Madame?*"

**Comment allez-vous, Madame?** *(French): How do you do, Madame?*

"Who the devil are you?" came the reply. The voice was only too familiar. And I smelled tea tree oil.

"Who am I!" Madame said testily. "Why,

wasn't it you, Madame, who invited me here? I am Madame Toutou Moucher, of course, and what's more I have been waiting nearly — hey! Where are you going? Why, how terribly rude!"

The hatch burst open.

"Mama!" Faith gasped.

"Get out of there this instant!" Bernice ordered, her face bright red.

"Mama, we're just about to blast off!"

"Faith! I have no patience for this! Get out!"

"I can't! It'll go up pilotless!"

The flame reached the fuel tank and disappeared inside it.

I whined.

"Mama!" Faith yelled. "In or out!"

The engine ignited and the *Peahen* began to shake.

**Grourgurg!**
*(Arf): Earthquake!*

Daphne awoke. *"Grourgurg!"* she howled.

Alex jumped up from his chair in a panic. "Let me out of here!" he hollered. The vibration bounced him off the wall and onto the floor beside me.

Bernice fell into his chair.

"Cri-mi-mi-nit-nit-nit-aly!" she yelled at Faith.

♦ ♦ ♦

The engine's roar during blast-off was, as usual, earsplitting, the vibration, teeth-rattling. This was becoming a bit old hat to me.

We all tried to maintain our positions. None succeeded. With so many of us in so small a space, it's not surprising we all became tangled up with one another. I seemed to have a peculiar attraction to Bernice. The feeling was not mutual.

At the usual altitude the rumbling abated and objects in the ship came to rest. We began to level off. Faith and Bernice found themselves in each other's arms. I found myself on Alex's head.

"I've really got to install seat belts," Faith said.

"Faith!" Bernice breathed. Her face was as white as a bone. She grasped her daughter's face in her hands.

"It's all right, Mama," Faith said through

puckered lips. "Blast-offs are always a little shaky. Look out the window. We're fine."

Bernice peeked out the window. Clouds streamed by.

"Criminitaly!" she gasped.

"Let me see!" Alex demanded, and started to nudge Bernice aside.

Bernice glowered at him. "Excuse me?" she said tersely. "Haven't you got any manners? Who are you, anyway?"

"That's Alex Wao, Mama," Faith explained.

"Well, at last we meet," Bernice said. "I think you'd be best advised, Mr. Wao, to employ some manners, regardless of where you are."

"Yes, ma'am," Alex said contritely. "Excuse me, ma'am. May I see out the window, please?"

"That's more like it," Bernice said. "You may."

Alex scrambled to the window and gazed out.

*"Ai ya!"* he said.

**Ai ya!** *(Chinese): Wow!*

Faith's face was bathed in glory.

It was then that I felt the *Peahen* shudder strangely, then cough.

*Something's wrong,* I wrote on an errant sheet of paper, then passed it to the captain.

Daphne gasped. "You wrote!" she said.

"What do you mean, Eddie?" Faith said.

*Can't you feel it?* I wrote.

"How do you do that?" Daphne insisted.

"Keep quiet!" Bernice snapped at Daphne.

"Who does she think she is?" Daphne growled.

"Whose dog is that?" Bernice asked Faith. "It looks sick."

"That's Daphne," Faith explained to Bernice. "A friend of Eddie's."

"That's my master's mother," I explained to Daphne. "She doesn't much care for dogs."

The ship coughed again.

"What's wrong, old girl?" Faith said to her rocket.

"Maybe the engine's dying," Alex said, his face draining of color.

"Did you do something?" Faith said crossly. She gave him a shove.

"Faith!" Bernice shouted. "That is unacceptable!"

"Why don't you check the fuel?" Alex said with a sob in his voice.

Faith reached for the handle on the fuel tank door. It opened without having to be turned.

"I didn't lock it!" she gasped.

"Is that bad?" Bernice asked.

Faith peered into the tank and shrieked. "It's empty!"

Alex and Bernice leaned over and looked in, too.

"You did this!" Faith snapped at Alex.

"You left it unlocked!" Alex said. "Not me!"

"You took the fuel out! I filled it this morning!"

"Maybe it burned away!" Alex said. A tear ran down his cheek.

"Not this fast!" Faith yelled. She punched him in the chest. "You did it! I hate you!" She was crying, too.

"Faith!" Bernice screamed. She placed her hand on her daughter's chest and pressed her back onto her chair. She looked straight into her eyes.

"It doesn't matter what happened," she said. "What can we do now?"

Faith stared at her shoes.

"Faith! This is no time to sulk!" Bernice said, when, suddenly the *Peahen*'s engine seized, hiccuped, and then died.

Faith's eyes grew wide. She rose to her feet. She puffed out her chest. She was captain again.

"Man the parachutes!" she commanded.

# The Tan Sea

# 16

If Faith had mentioned parachutes during her systems check, I hadn't noticed. Of course, there would have been no reason for me to notice — the word would have meant nothing to me. I only learned the meaning of "parachute" at the point when I was dangling below one, my four paws frantically pawing at nothing but air.

I thought of the dream I'd had in Bernice's fuchsia bed.

Faith had loaded four parachutes aboard the ship — two for rocket kids, two for rocket dogs. She had not counted on having along a rocket Mama.

"You take mine!" she yelled to Bernice. "I'll go with Eddie!"

"I don't like this!" Bernice yelled back.

"Put it on, Mama!" Faith yelled. She tossed a chute to Bernice, then began harnessing me up.

Bernice reluctantly did as her daughter bade. Alex hurriedly slipped on his chute. He tied his straps in triple knots.

After Faith had finished with me, she moved toward Daphne. Daphne flattened her ears and snarled.

"Let her put it on you!" I yapped in Arf.

Faith looked into Daphne's eyes and smiled. "It's all right, widdle wuppler!" she yelled. "I won't hurt you!"

She put her hand up close to Daphne's snout. I was surprised by her boldness. Having once felt the awful sting of one of Daphne's nips, I could not help but fear for the worst. But Daphne did not nip. She sniffed. Then she stuck out her tongue and licked my master's fingertips. She licked and licked and licked. I like to think that Faith had won her trust, but, in truth, she probably just had some pig fat under her nails.

When Faith had finished suiting up Daphne, she pulled on her own pack, then knelt down beside me. She pressed her mouth up to my ear.

"I'm going to strap myself to you, Eddie," she said. "I hope that's all right."

**Ow groo!**
***(Bowwow): That's fine!***

*"Ow groo!"* I howled. I was glad not to go alone.

"Faith!" Bernice yelled. "Hurry!"

Faith quickly told me how to operate the parachute, then said to relay the instructions to Daphne, which I did. Daphne just snarled. I wished her good luck anyway and gave her a lick on the flews. In case I never saw her again, I wanted to have done so. I felt a familiar tingle on my tongue: jalapeños! Had she . . . ?

"Let's go!" Faith yelled.

She opened the hatch. It blew open and banged against the side of the ship. This was the second time we would be bailing out of the *Peahen*, dear reader. The first time — in the first story — we landed in the Pacific Ocean. I crept to the opening and looked down. Below was what appeared to be a tan sea.

"I'll go last!" Bernice yelled to Faith. "Go!"

"Geronimo!" Faith hollered, and pushed off.

To my surprise, jumping out of the *Peahen* gave me more a feeling of going up than down. Though I'm certain it was an illusion, it felt as if suddenly we were lighter than air. As if we were floating. But then, dramatically, the illusion vanished. We were falling — just as the *Peahen* was, just as rain does, and from just as high.

Faith's skirt blew upward and flapped against us. My ears and flews flapped as well. Faith reached her hand around my belly and poked her finger through an orange plastic ring on the harness. She gave it a yank. I heard a muffled fluttering sound — like a flock of *palomas* lifting off — and looked up to see a measure of silken orange fabric unfolding. It was tethered with cords to the harness.

**palomas** *(Spanish): doves; pigeons*

"Brace yourself!" Faith shouted and tightened her grip.

A second later, the harness jerked. I tasted *shumei* on my tongue. The feeling of floating returned. This time it was no illusion. I resumed breathing. I hadn't even noticed I had stopped.

The *Peahen* fell away, its size and noise diminishing as it dropped. I spotted small, bright orange circles in the distance. One, two, three.

"I don't like this!" Faith yelled in my ear. "Look how far away we are from the others!"

She was right. We were scattering.

"It's the wind!" Faith shouted.

It ruffled the parachute. It blew us back and forth under it like a pendulum. It propelled us farther and farther away from Bernice, Alex, and Daphne. It was hot. It eddied around us, blowing bits of grit into our faces. I tried to keep my mouth shut, but that's no easy thing for *Canis familiaris.* The grit tasted salty.

To my surprise, when we finally reached the tan surface, we sunk into it. It was sand. I was soon into it up to my brisket. The wind pushed it like waves across the surface, filling the air with its spray. The ground and the sky became almost indistinguishable. All was a swirling, stinging, sandy sea, its surf crashing over us.

"The desert!" Faith said, spitting out sand. "Oh swell! Just swell!"

The parachute settled down beside us, deflated, and began flopping about like a happy dog's tail. Faith yanked on its cords, hand over hand, and slowly the chute inched toward us. When she could reach the orange silk, she grabbed it and pulled it over us, tucking the edges underneath us.

"We'll have to wait until this dies down," Faith said, out of breath. "Then we'll look for the others."

She pulled a small canteen from her pack and poured some water into her cupped hand. I lapped it up. She repeated this process several times before she took a drink herself.

"What's this?" she asked, pulling Hector's book of poetry from the bag. "And this?" She pulled out the paper and pen.

I took the pen in my mouth, set the paper on the book, and wrote, Daphne ate the fuel.

"What?" Faith said. "Daphne?"

I nodded.

I smelled jalapeño on her breath, I wrote.

"Oh," Faith said. "I guess it wasn't Alex, then."

I shook my head.

To pass the time, Faith read poems to me from Hector's book. Outside, the wind continued to howl and whine. At times it sounded almost canine. Sand continued to pelt the parachute. It gathered in heaps on the windward side. When it piled up too high, and threatened to pour over us, we scooted out from under it. On and on Faith read, sand heaped, and we scooted, until the light outside began to dim. When it dimmed so much that Faith could no longer see the words on the page, she pulled a flashlight out of her pack and flicked it on.

"'O, that you were yourself, but, love, you are,'" she read. (It was number XIII.) "'No longer yours than you yourself here live.'" Then she turned to me and said, "Huh?"

# Runaway Bunny

# 17

The sandstorm eventually wound down and died. We wormed our way out of our little dune and shook off the sand. The sky above had gone from beige to orange. The sun was gone. A flock of large black birds circled silently overhead. The powdery silhouettes of what seemed to be hundreds of sand dunes lay scattered around us.

"Swell," Faith sighed.

I sneezed sand out my nostrils, then took a deep, fact-finding breath. I smelled Faith. I smelled salt. And, ever so faintly, I smelled dog. I did not, however, smell *laurel.*

"Can you smell the others?" asked Faith.

I shook my head. A little sand fell in a mist from my dewlap.

"Any ideas which way to go?" she asked.

I only had the one lead — the dog smell. It wasn't Daphne, but if Harry Swift was right — if dogs really were created for human beings — then following the smell might just lead us to people.

**Hoo-ark!**
*(Bowwow): This way!*

*"Hoo-ark!"* I said, and started off toward it. Faith packed our gear and ran to catch up.

The sky shifted from orange to vermilion to violet to indigo. There was no moon. The light of the stars, outshone all day by the big, bright, close sun, now had the sky to themselves. I was grateful they were up there. They had a way of making the desert seem less unfamiliar.

The night air was cold and dry. I have never known such thirst! We emptied the contents of Faith's canteen in no time at all. My rather inefficient manner of drinking sent a goodly portion of the precious fluid to the sandy ground, I'm sad to say. Canteens were clearly not designed with dogs in mind.

Then, to make matters worse, that confounded scent I was tracking kept eluding me. Just as I thought I had a bead on it, it would vanish. A moment later it would reappear, wafting in from some other direction. But then, once I'd fixed on it again, again it disappeared. After this had happened a dozen times or so, I began to suspect that Faith and I were traveling in circles. What's more, I had a sinking feeling that maybe the hound out there had just this in mind.

"Eddie," Faith said in a heavy voice. "I'm pooped."

She plopped down on her bottom in the sand. I licked her face with my dry tongue. Her skin was cold.

"Are you cold?" she asked me, shivering. "I thought deserts were hot."

I curled up beside her. She opened the parachute and wrapped it around us.

"Are you hungry?" she asked.

I nodded.

"Me, too," she said. "All I brought were *chicles*. I didn't expect this to happen." Her teeth were chattering.

I nuzzled up closer and gave her chin a lick.

"Do you want a *chicle*?" she asked.

Just then the wind changed course and I caught scent of something. It was rodent. I raised my head.

"What is it?" Faith whispered.

A moment later, another scent appeared. At first I thought it was the dog smell, but it was a far more charming scent than that! It was *laurel*!

"Lorl!" I howled. "Lorl!"

And, suddenly, there in the distance, surmounting a dune in great haste, appeared a small gray hare. A split second later, Daphne topped the dune! Oh, she was alive! She was alive!

In fact, she looked extremely alive. Her head, neck, and back curved in an elegant arc, her ears were tucked back, her muscular legs pumped in perfect concert. She cut through the air like an arrow, like a swallow, like a shaft of light. She was magnificent!

The poor bunny didn't stand a chance. It stumbled as it rushed down a steep dune and Daphne swooped in for the kill. She snatched it in her jaws, and with a swift snap of her head, ended the little thing's life.

"Lorl!" I called again.

She raised her head and cocked it in our direction. The rabbit hung limply in her mouth.

"Daphne!" Faith called. "Here, girl!"

Daphne's tail began to wag. My feeling was that she was not so much truly glad to see us as she was glad that someone had seen *her*, and paid witness to her hitherto hidden hunting prowess. She strutted proudly over to us and laid the bloodied carcass at Faith's feet.

"Ew!" Faith said, sticking her tongue out. "Gross!"

# The Dog Star

# 18

"Go ahead," Daphne said to me. "Dig in."

Her black eyes glistened. She breathed heavily through her mouth, her breath saturated with the scent of hare. The desert had not taken the same toll on her as it had on us. She radiated.

"No, you first," I insisted.

"I've eaten," she said, beaming. Obviously, this had not been her first kill.

I bit into the hare's hind and began gnawing. It was my first taste of rabbit and set me to thinking how my time abroad had certainly opened me up to new experiences, cuisine-wise.

"Ask her if she's seen Bernice or Alex," Faith said to me.

I left off the meat momentarily and asked.

“I haven’t seen them,” Daphne answered.

“Dang it,” Faith said before I could translate.

I had that feeling again. The feeling that she’d understood.

“They don’t have food or water, Eddie,” Faith said, lying back onto the sand. “Mama hates camping.”

I looked down at the femur I had been so blithely stripping clean and realized that not only Bernice and Alex lacked food and water. Faith hadn’t eaten, either, and I knew there was no way she was going to eat raw rabbit. I buried the femur in the sand and snuggled up next to my master, my snout on her chest.

“I hope they’re together,” she said to the sky. “I hope she’s not too mad.”

The stars just twinkled silently.

“Well, I sure showed Alex, didn’t I?” Faith said in a sarcastic tone. “Who knows where he is, or if he’s all right.”

I looked up into her eyes. They were filled with regret.

"Why did I do it, Eddie?" she said. "*I* knew the *Peahen* could fly. Why did I care that he didn't believe me? What does *he* know?"

I knew she was right, of course, because I had done the same thing. Why hadn't I trusted myself? Why hadn't I had the patience to allow Daphne to learn about me in her own way, at her own pace? Why did I feel I needed to trick her aboard a rocket ship to prove to her that I'm worthwhile?

"I didn't like the way he teased me all the time," Faith said softly. "Ms. Ng always told me, 'Don't play with him if he's not nice to you.' So did Mama." She sighed. My head rose with her belly, then slowly sank back down. "Maybe I just like him anyway," she said.

Hearing that, I vowed to myself to give Alex more of a chance, boy or not. If I wanted Daphne to look past my electricity — past my scraggly coat to the dog within — shouldn't I be just as open-minded with Alex? Of course, this depended on whether or not I would ever see him again. I found myself hoping that I would.

"We weren't in the air very long," Faith said in

a more matter-of-fact voice. "We're probably still in California. I think this might be Death Valley," she said.

I didn't like the sound of that.

"There's the Dog Star," she said, pointing. "That one. The brightest one."

I looked up.

"It's chasing the Hare," she said. "That little star. That's the Hare."

I saw the ones she meant.

"Just like Daphne," she said. "Chasing the hare."

Daphne, who had been combing the area for more prey, trotted over and curled up on the other side of Faith. Probably heard her name. Faith gave her the whole treatment — the rubbing, the scratching, the cooing. Daphne purred. I've yet to meet a pooch who can resist Faith's handiwork.

"Tell her I'm not mad about the fuel," Faith said to me. "It's okay. I understand."

I considered whether or not to tell Daphne what she'd done. I doubted that she had made a connection between her eating of the pig fat and our current predicament. How could she have known that one had brought on the other? I decided it didn't really matter. There was no sense in pointing toes. Besides, as much as I truly wished she hadn't eaten the fuel, how could I hold it against her? On the contrary, her porklust made her all the more attractive to me. Actually, my concern was more that she was angry at *me* for getting her into this mess.

"Are you sore at me?" I asked her.

"About what?" she asked.

"All this," I said. "The rocket. The crash. Being stuck here."

"Are you kidding?" she said. "It was exciting! I loved the rocket! I even loved the falling! It was like flying! And I've never caught a rabbit before! I've never had the chance!"

"We didn't plan to bail out, you know," I said. "Something went wrong with the ship."

"I understand," she said. "These things happen."

I nodded.

"I thought *you'd* be angry," she said.

"About what?" I asked.

"I haven't been very nice to you," she said.

"Oh, that," I said, waving a paw. "Don't give it another thought."

"I don't know what gets into me," she said. "It's the training, I suppose."

"The training?"

"The obedience school. And the charm school. You know, for the runway."

"The runway?"

"I'm a competitor," she said. "A show dog."

"Oh," I said. I recalled a picture of a whippet wearing a medal in the dog book in Dante's bookshop.

"Reserve is a quality much admired in the show," she said. "The judges like a turned-up snout."

"Like your master's," I said.

"Yes, like Sniff's," Daphne said. She said *sniff* by sniffing. In Arf, *sniff* means "snob."

"That's what you call her?" I said.

"To her face," Daphne said, grinning.

**sniff** *(Arf):* *snob*

"But you both act the same," I said, and then wished that I hadn't. "I mean —"

"You're right," she said. "I'm a bit of a *sniff.* Especially around her. Like I said, it's the training."

"Don't you like the dog shows?"

"I like hunting rabbits better," she said, laying a paw on her heart. "Oh!" she said suddenly as if she'd just thought of something. She fumbled at her sweater pocket. "You left something at my house."

"I did?"

And what do you think she dug out of her sweater pocket, dear reader?

"My poem!" I barked.

"You had it in your mouth that last night you came to my house," she said. Then she leaned in a little nearer and spoke in a more somber tone. "I saw you — up there in the rocket. I saw you. You can write." She set the poem on Faith's belly. "Will you read it to me?"

A kind of panic overcame me. I'd written it before I really knew her. Now that I'd seen her kill, I wasn't so sure it would be her cup of tea.

"Please?" she asked, nudging the paper toward me.

I studied her face. It did not seem the least bit supercilious. It looked friendly. I checked her tail. It was curved outward, and wagging.

"You won't laugh?" I said. "You might find it silly."

"I won't laugh," she said with a smile.

"I wanted you to like me," I said.

She nosed the poem closer to me. "Read it," she said.

I turned the poem around the right way. The stars, if you can believe it, shone so brightly, that, even without a moon, I could make out the words.

"Go on," she said, nudging my neck with her narrow nose. "Read."

I cleared my throat, then, in a trembling voice, I read:

# Bird Dog

♦ ♦ ♦ ♦ ♦ ♦ ♦ ♦ ♦

# 19

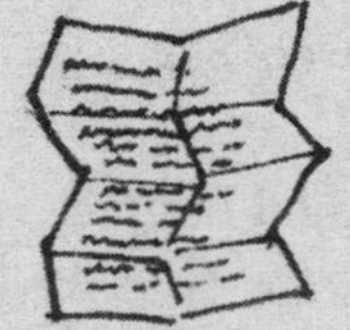

If at dawn upon my back
I find the wings I've always lacked
and so the sky becomes my den
and to the sun I soar
and then

it's back to earth and you, my love,
to show you how from dog a dove
has come to take you high above
where, free from leash and tick and flea,
you'll gambol in a cloudy sea
and want for naught
except for me.

But if at dawn you are not blessed
with feathered limbs upon your crest
but worse you find you are bereft

of leg and paw, both right and left,
and really are more slug than dog
(as stationary as a log)
and realize that you *can't* fly —
it won't do any good to try —
and resigned you are to lie and lie
and lie and dwell beneath the sky,

then I will gladly stay
earthbound
and build our love nest
on the ground.

# The Slightest Slurp

♦ ♦ ♦ ♦ ♦

# 20

**hipos**
***(Spanish):***
***the hiccups***

**colibri**
***(Spanish):***
***hummingbird***

**cocodrilo**
***(Spanish):***
***crocodile***

**fruffruff**
***(Bowwow):***
***little parrot***

I happen to like words very much. I like reading them, writing them, speaking them, listening to them. I like hearing them sung. Some are silly, like "chinchilla," "gobbledygook," and "pizzazz." Others are positively nutty — for example, "frogwort," "jipijapa," "kookaburra." Some suit their meanings to a tee. The sneeze is well-named, as are the clarinet, the platypus, and *hipos.* "Supercilious" really sounds like what it means: hissy.

Other words delight for more inexplicable reasons. I happen to like "plum" very much. I can't say why. I just do. And I love the "ling" words, like "bristling," "nibbling," and "tickling." I'm also quite fond of *colíbri* and *cocodrilo.* They're so melodious. And I love to say the word *fruffruff* — though I rarely get the chance.

But there is one word, dear reader, that, for me, dwarfs all others. It is a word among words. In sound, in shape, in meaning, it is peerless. Crisp and whispery, with just the right blend of clickiness and slinky sibilance. It is an English word, that, alas, I cannot speak.

It's "kiss."

You may think dogs don't kiss, per se. True, we don't pucker and pop. But we kiss. Actually, we slurp. I prefer to think of it as kissing.

♦ ♦ ♦

She kissed me. After the poem. Just a little one — the slightest slurp — on the jaw.

The rewards of writing are rich.

# Superciliousness

♦ ♦ ♦ ♦ ♦ ♦ ♦ ♦ ♦ ♦ ♦ ♦ ♦ ♦ ♦ ♦

# 21

It was then, dear reader, as we stole a moment of comfort from a day of misadventure, that I first heard the beast that I had, up to then, only sniffed. I smelled the tricky desert dog. And I heard howling.

The language was unknown to me, yet hauntingly familiar. Something about it reminded me of Bowwow. In fact, it also bore more than a passing resemblance to Arf, and even to Ruff, the house dog dialect of San Cristóbal de las Casas. This is not altogether surprising once you stop to consider that Bowwow, Arf, and Ruff are very probably distant cousins, in much the same way that, say, French, Spanish, and Italian are. So even though this strange desert canine howled in a tongue I did not know, I permitted myself to believe that I understood it. This was not really such a huge leap of faith, considering, after all, the dog was just howling. Howling dogs are almost always saying the same thing: "I'm here; I'm alone; I'm hungry," or some variation on this theme. Whether or not one finds oneself in similar circumstances, it is considered in canine circles right and proper to respond. After all, all of us, at one time or another, have been there.

*"Bu-rooo!"* I howled.

*"Ee-row!"* Daphne howled.

"What is it?" Faith said, sitting up.

*"Oo ur,"* I said, without considering to whom I was speaking.

"What kind?" Faith asked.

I squinted at her. I had that feeling again, that hunch that she understood.

"Not 'dog,'" came a distant voice from the dark. "Not hardly."

Daphne growled.

"Who are you?" I asked. I spoke in Arf, think-

**Bu-rooo!**
***(Bowwow):***
***I'm here!***

**Ee-row!**
***(Arf):***
***I'm here!***

**Oo ur**
***(Bowwow):***
***A dog***

ing that, if we were still in the United States — as Faith seemed to think — it would be the language the dog would most likely know.

"I am not a dog," the voice said. "Thank heavens."

"Do you understand him?" Daphne whispered to me.

I nodded. "It's a new language to me, but I think I get most of it. He clearly understands me."

"Clearly," the voice said. Then it snickered.

"We're lost," I said to the voice. "We've been separated from our friends. Two humans. Have you seen them?"

The animal just snickered again.

"Will you take us to them?" I asked.

Snicker.

"Please!" I whined.

But the scent had gone.

"It's gone," Daphne said. For a sight hound, her nose wasn't bad.

"Probably a coyote," Faith said. "Coyotes live in the desert."

I thought back to our conversation about wild dogs, how Faith had said that domesticated dogs were bred from wolves, foxes, hyenas, jackals — and coyotes.

I unzipped the pack and pulled out paper and pen. Phrasing it as delicately as I could, I wrote, Do coyotes harm people?

"No," Faith said. "They eat small animals. Rodents. Insects. Mostly, they scavenge."

Like street dogs, I thought.

"They eat carrion," Faith continued. "Dead things." Suddenly she stared intently at me. "Why?" she said. "Do you think Mama and Alex might be in danger?"

It had crossed my mind. But I really couldn't say for sure. I'd had no experience with coyotes then.

"Right," Faith said. "Let's go." She stood and began bundling up the parachute. I sat motionless, surprised by the suddenness of her action. "Now!" she barked.

I jumped to my feet.

“Ma-ma!” Faith yelled as we walked. She cupped her hands around her mouth. “Al-ex! Ma-ah-ma!”

*“Ee-row!”* Daphne called.

*“Bu-rooo!”* I echoed.

**Ooo-rooo! Ooo-rrr!**
***(Yowl): I’m here! I’m hungry!***

*“Ooo-rooo! Ooo-rrr!”* answered the voice from the darkness.

# Lulus

# 22

"That's final!" Faith said sharply. "You are *not* to go up in that rocket ship ever again!"

"Who's she talking to?" Daphne whispered to me.

"Herself," I said. "She's imagining what her mother will say when we find her."

"*This* is what happens, missy, when you don't do as you're told!" Faith went on. "Criminitaly! I just wish that once, just *once*, you would listen to me!"

"Her mother will be angry?" Daphne asked.

"That'd be my guess," I said.

"But why?" Daphne said. "You'd think she'd be grateful! I love it here! It's paradise!"

I understood how she felt. I had felt the same

way at first on Bone Island. Away from the cars and the boys, out in the wild, where a dog could be predator, instead of prey or pet. Where a dog could choose its own territory, and mark it. Where a dog could be free. In the end, though, I eagerly left Bone Island. Freedom, I have learned, is not out there somewhere, waiting to be found. It's always with you. Like your tail.

I did not love being in the desert. Its sands concealed what Faith most needed to see — her mother and her friend. It pained me to see how she despaired. Her body, her mind, and her spirit had become beaten and weary. She was losing hope.

I appealed silently to the Dog Star for help.

"Dog Star," I prayed. "I once read that all living things on earth contain within them the material of stars. That makes us kin. As stars. As dogs. We're electric. I need your help.

"I know that your light comes from very far away. Years away, in fact. Do you exist in the future? Do you know how things will turn out?

If you do, could you somehow let on to Faith that everything will be all right? She's terribly upset."

The stars just glimmered as before. I imagined that their glimmering was their language, and wished that I understood it. I determined to pay more attention, and try to pick it up.

"Do you smell that?" Daphne said suddenly.

I sniffed.

"Coyote?" Faith asked.

It wasn't coyote. It was animal, of that I was sure. A mammal. I was even fairly sure which species. But I wouldn't accept what my nose told me. What it said just couldn't be — not there, not out in the middle of the desert. But a dog's nose doesn't lie.

"It's a —" Daphne began, then sniffed again. "Isn't it?"

"I'm almost certain," I said.

"I don't understand," Faith said. "What is it?"

I could have dug out paper and pen and written it for her. I was beginning to think that I could just bark it to her and she'd understand. But I decided to wait and see if Daphne and I were right. I couldn't really see what difference it would make either way. Right or wrong, I couldn't see how it would bring us any closer to our goal — how it would bring us any nearer to Bernice and Alex. Still, it was something to go on. My instinct told me to track it down.

"I say we hunt it down," Daphne said.

The scent led us across the dunes to a mound of large stones. Up until then, we'd seen only sand and occasional scrub, so the sight of the stones alone was a welcome relief. But there was more. At the base of the mound was a dense patch of brambles. Daphne and I nosed our way through it toward the source of the smell, and there, with two large stones as a lintel, lay the entrance to a cave.

Daphne sniffed. "Whatever it is," she said, "it went in there. And recently."

Suddenly I heard Faith call out. *"Lulu!"* was what she called.

"What's she saying?" Daphne asked.

I shook my head. I didn't know. The word held no meaning for me in any of my languages — not in Bowwow or Arf, not in Miau or Mew or Yiaow, not in English or Spanish, French or Italian or German, Tzotzil or Tzeltal or Mixtec, Japanese or Chinese (which, admittedly, I was then only learning). Not even in Widdlish. Needless to say, my curiosity was piqued. I began making my way back out through the tangle.

*"Lulu!"* Faith kept calling. *"Lulu! Lulu! Lulu!"*

When at last I was free, I raced toward the sound of my master's voice. It led me around to the other side of the mound of stones. There, I found her kneeling beside a small, tin rocket ship lying on its side in the sand.

It was not the *Peahen.*

"It's the *Lulu,*" Faith said quietly.

The rocket was much smaller than the *Peahen.* A person could not have fit inside it, not even a small person. I doubted that even a medium-sized dog, even a skinny one, like a whippet, or myself, could have.

Letters were painted on the little rocket's side. They were cracked and peeling. I made out an L, a J — or was it a U? Then an I, or maybe it was another L . . .

*"Lulu,"* Faith said yet again.

And that is what was written there: L-U-L-U.

"That's me," Faith said. A tear formed in the corner of her eye. "I'm Lulu."

♦ ♦ ♦

Luisa Faith Urquhart-Brindisi. That's my master's full name. Her father, Babbo, was Luigi Brindisi — a fun name to say, I would think: Loo-EE-gee Brin-DEE-zee. Luigi had many pet names for his daughter. One of them he derived from Luisa, her actual first name. He simply doubled the first syllable: Lulu.

"He built this rocket for me," Faith said. "We were going to take it out to the middle of nowhere and launch it with some of my stuffed animals aboard. It has a parachute so that they could come back down all right. But then, before we got a chance to, he found out he was sick."

I licked away her tear when it fell.

"After he died, we couldn't find it. Mama said he must have sold it, but I didn't believe it. He made it for me. He named it after me. He wouldn't have sold it."

Her next words matched my thoughts verbatim: "How do you think it got here?"

"Grumph!" Daphne barked from within the brush. I'd almost forgotten about her! Imagine that!

*"Ee-row, Lorl!"* I howled back.

"Maybe she found something," Faith said.

We left the *Lulu* and ran to the edge of the brambles.

"Where have you been?" Daphne called out. "What's it all about?"

"I found the *Lulu*!" Faith shouted, up on her toes.

She was doing it again! Answering!

"I'll explain later," I called to Daphne. "Did you find anything?"

"I went in the cave a ways," Daphne called back. "It looks very dangerous. It's pitch-black."

"We have the flashlight," Faith said to me.

That was the clincher! She knew what we were saying!

She knew Arf!

**Rowr froo?**
***(Arf): Where is it?***

*"Rowr froo?"* I asked, just to test her.

"In the pack," she answered. She pulled off her backpack and began to unzip it.

"You understand me," I said. I looked her in the eyes. "You understand Arf."

She stopped unzipping and looked at me. I don't think she'd realized it yet. Maybe, like me, she picks up languages without even trying. She'd certainly learned Spanish readily enough — once she decided she could. And some Italian and Chinese . . .

"Yes," she said. "I do, don't I?" She smiled. "Say something else!"

Oh, that pressure again! Don't you hate it? I went for the sentimental.

*"Grumph rroof-roof,"* I said.

"Aw, I love you, too, pupplers," she said, and kissed my snout.

It was confirmed. I remember thinking how ironic it was that her first dog language was not *my* first dog language, just as the first human language I learned — Spanish — was not her first human language. She understood Arf, not Bowwow. She must have picked it up listening to Daphne and me. Oh, well. It wasn't such a leap from one to the other.

Faith dug the flashlight out of her bag. "Let's go in," she said.

Unfortunately, she was not going to be able to join us. The thicket was too thick, especially up at her level. The cave was too narrow. I told her so. She did not like it.

"We'll be right back," I said. "Just wait by the rocket ship for us."

She grumbled, but complied. Masters don't like to be mastered.

**Grumph rroof-roof** *(Arf): I love you*

I crawled in through the brambles to Daphne.

"What's going on?" she asked.

"Never mind," I said. "I'll tell you later."

I shone the light down into the cave. It looked cramped and spooky.

"Well, one of us should probably stay out here," Daphne said. "With your master."

Then one of us said, "I'll go in."

Guess, dear reader, which one.

# The First Girl in Space

◆ ◆ ◆ ◆ ◆ ◆ ◆ ◆

# 23

Once inside the cave, a strong, putrid stench hit my nostrils. I recognized it easily enough: guano, bat dung. Nothing else smells quite like it. I shone the beam on the wall and saw a dark, oozy substance clinging there. Guano, all right. Though I'm aware that most people wrinkle their nose up at the scent of it, I actually find its stench to be delightful — delectable, even. But, then, dear reader, you should consider the source.

In the beginning, the cave was tall enough and wide enough for me to move along it without much encumbrance. I passed many forks in the path as I went. My only way of choosing was by nose: I followed the scent — the one I'd come in after — which mingled in the air with the guano and the musty smell of damp stone. In time, though, the cave grew so narrow I could feel its clammy walls grazing my sides. I could feel the guano. The floor of the cave began to gradually trend downward. It became pitted and craggy. Occasionally, I came across gaping holes in the floor that, had I not had Faith's light, I would not have known about. I shuddered to think on it.

But then, just when I thought the tunnel had shrunk one size too many for me, and I would be stuck like Winnie-the-Pooh in Rabbit's rabbit hole (I love Pooh), I suddenly found myself in a large, open chamber. Massive stone cones hung from the ceiling. Others rose up from the floor. The only sound was the echoey drip, drip, drip of water droplets falling into scattered puddles on the floor. I sniffed out the gnawed remains of a bat. Only its wings, head, and spine were left. It had not died a natural death.

The scent I was after was now stronger than ever.

A bat screeched and, as it flapped by overhead, I heard a hiss. It came from behind a cone. When

I shone the light over, I saw a whisker. Two red circles of light glowed. I sniffed and realized that Daphne and I had been right.

We'd smelled cat.

*"Hssss!"* the cat said.

**Hssss!**
***(Mew):***
***Get lost!***

I slung my head low and moved slowly toward it.

"I know that smell," the cat murmured, almost inaudibly.

I pricked up my ears.

"It's the smell of my master's child," it purred.

I moved in closer and it edged out further from behind its hiding place. I saw a paw, a leg, a tail — the entire cat.

It was purplish. (Faith would say bluish.)

♦ ♦ ♦

Valentina Vladimirovna Nikolayeva Tereshkova. The first girl in space. Though there had to be a connection between Luigi's cat and Luigi's rocket both being in a desert far from San Francisco, I was not about to make it.

Perhaps, dear reader, you'd like a shot at it.

I remember then being struck suddenly with a deep and abiding respect for the *Peahen*. It seemed to me quite likely that she was possessed of some sort of genius for knowing just where it was we needed to go. This should not be confused with where we *wanted* to go. I began to think that she was more than pounded tin and rivets, that maybe she knew languages — languages of the clouds, maybe, or of the sky, or even of the stars, languages that led her to the places that would best prove to us that rocket ships don't solve anything.

I wanted, of course, to inform Veevy that Faith was waiting just outside the cave, but I couldn't. As I've mentioned, I understand Mew, but cannot speak it. I doubted seriously that Veevy could speak or understand any dog languages. I'd never met a cat who could. Aside from myself, I've never known a dog who could understand a cat. Still, I had nothing to lose. I spoke softly so as not to frighten her.

"Your master's child is outside," I said in Arf.

(As with the coyote, I thought Arf would be the dog language to which she would probably have had the most exposure.)

*"Hssss!"* Veevy replied, and shrank back into her hiding place.

We couldn't communicate. That was plain. No wonder relations between dogs and cats are so strained.

I decided to just head back, hoping she would follow. I'd heard it said before that cats are curious. Unfortunately, I soon discovered that heading back proved to be a much knottier proposal than I had anticipated. All those forks in the road on the way in became forks again — in reverse — on the way out. I did not, this time, have a scent to guide me. What's more, I had been so single-minded in my pursuit of the scent, I had neglected to stop off from time to time and leave my mark. Daphne's scent would have been a good beacon, but she had probably joined Faith by the *Lulu*, and so was well out of noseshot. All I could smell was the guano and the cat and stone. I was lost.

I have no idea how long I wandered down in that catacomb. An hour. Two. Three. I really can't say. Maybe it was ten minutes. All I know is that, at some point, the beam of my flashlight dimmed, flickered, and then went out.

Being in darkness has never really bothered me. A scent hound relies very little on his vision. But standing there, underground, in pitch-blackness, far from home and Faith and even the stars, I felt lost in a way that had nothing to do with my senses. I felt lost to the world, like a treasure chest at the bottom of the blackest sea.

*"Bu-rooo!"* I howled. *"Bu-rooo!"*

**Mee-yoo**
*(Mew):*
*I'm here*

*"Mee-yoo,"* Veevy said from somewhere.

She pussyfooted up to me and grazed my leg. *"Hrrr,"* she said. Then she padded quickly away. I followed her scent. She led me along through the maze, mewing from time to time to see if I was keeping up. *"Bu-rooo,"* I'd say, and she'd answer, *"Mee-yoo,"* and continue on.

**Hrrr**
*(Mew):*
*Nice*

Finally, puffing and panting and dying for open air, I reached the opening. Never have I relished the sight of the stars so much! And the moon was up — big and round and smiling!

And there was the *Lulu*!

But how did it get here, I thought, so close to the cave opening? It had been around the other side of the mound of stones. And it was so big!

And then I realized — it wasn't the *Lulu* at all.

# Mama Mia!

♦ ♦ ♦ ♦ ♦ ♦ ♦ ♦ ♦ ♦ ♦ ♦ ♦

# 24

"That was not there before," Veevy said as the two of us approached the ship. "It looks like mine." She padded over to it. "It's huge!"

The *Peahen* stood upright in the sand. This puzzled me. What was the likelihood that an unmanned spacecraft crashing to earth would land nose up? What's more, she showed no sign whatsoever of having just gone through what must have been a dreadful crash landing. She was in remarkable shape, almost as good as before the launch.

"I smell something," the cat purred softly. "Something from long ago."

I did, too. I clambered up the side of the rocket and peered in the porthole. The scent increased.

It was tea tree oil!

"What does he see?" Veevy mewed.

I saw Alex, asleep, his head on Bernice's lap!

Bernice jerked her head in my direction. "Go away, coyote!" she screamed, and threw something at the porthole. It struck the pane with a thump.

Obviously she mistook me for someone else. I jumped down from the window and tried to pull open the hatch. It was locked.

*"Ow Grumph!"* I said.

**Ow Grumph!** ***(Bowwow): It's me!***

"Edison?" Bernice said faintly. Her face appeared in the porthole.

"It's the evil one!" Veevy shrieked.

The hatch swung open and Bernice climbed out. She fell to her knees in the sand beside me. Her face was worn by hours of worry. I jumped to my feet and licked it.

"Stop it! Stop it!" she said, pushing me away. "Where's Faith?"

But then suddenly, as if she had been smacked sharply on the nose, her head snapped backward. She scooted back away from me.

"Criminitaly, Edison!" she said bringing her

hand over her nose and mouth. "What have you been *into*?"

I looked down at myself. My coat was caked with guano. I smiled embarrassedly, then dropped to the ground and began rolling around in the sand. The sand was too loose, however, and the guano too gluey for this to have any real effect. I ended up looking like the contents of a litter box.

Bernice squeezed her nose with her fingers. "Never mind," she said. "Just tell me where Faith is."

I made a gesture with my snout — a writing gesture.

"Right!" she said and jumped to her feet. She ducked into the *Peahen* and reemerged a moment later with Faith's systems-check clipboard. She flipped the checklist over and handed me the pen, which was chained to the board.

"No coyotes?" a voice said tremulously. I looked up to see Alex poking his head out of the hatch.

"No, Alex," Bernice said. "It's only Edison." Then to me, she said, "Well?"

Alex inched his way over and stood behind Bernice. His eyes kept darting about as if expecting to see something fearful.

"What stinks?" he said, wrinkling up his nose.

Faith's fine, I wrote. She's with Daphne.

"He's writing!" Alex yelped.

"Quiet, please, Alex," Bernice said, in a surprisingly patient way. "Where is she, Edison?"

I'm not sure, I wrote, then winced.

Bernice took a deep breath and let it out.

"Is he really a dog?" Alex said, leaning over and trying to look in my mouth. "Hello?" he called inside. But then, just as Bernice had, he recoiled. "It's him!" he said. "P.U.!" (I have never discovered what those initials stand for.)

"When did you last see her?" Bernice asked me.

I explained how I'd left Faith at the other opening of the cave, along with Daphne and the other rocket.

"Other rocket?" she asked.

I nodded. Luigi's, I wrote.

"Luigi's!" she said, bringing her hand to her mouth. "What do you mean? How do you know?"

It said "Lulu" on the side.

**Mama mia!** ***(Italian): My goodness!; literally, my mama***

*"Mama mia!"* Bernice said. She looked away, lost in thought. "I remember," she said to herself. "The rocket he named after Faith. We couldn't find it."

I have to admit, dear reader, that, up to then, in the back of my mind, I had wondered if perhaps — knowing Bernice's feelings for Veevy — she was somehow responsible for Veevy and the *Lulu* ending up out there in the desert together. Not a nice thought, I know, but, well, it added up. It was a relief, then, that she seemed genuinely surprised and confused.

It's here, I wrote.

"He understands you!" Alex said. "How does he do that?"

"I'll explain later, Alex," Bernice said to him.

"Yes, ma'am," Alex said. (I couldn't get over these two!)

Veevy's here, too, I wrote.

"Who's Veevy?" Bernice asked.

Luigi's cat, I wrote.

Just then Veevy, who had been hiding behind one of the *Peahen*'s fins, slithered out, her hackles up.

*"Hsss!"* Veevy said to Bernice. *"Hsss, yee-owr!"*

**yee-owr!** *(Mew): evil one*

"How did *she* get here?" Bernice gasped.

Poor Bernice. She'd had a lot of weird things to grapple with lately. A literate pet. A rocketeering daughter. An impromptu rocket ride. Parachutes. Coyotes. The *Lulu*. And now, Valentina Vladimirovna Nikolayeva Tereshkova. For a moment she appeared to be sorting it all out, coming to grips with it. But then, with a shake of her head, she just let it all go and retrained her focus on me.

"Can you lead us back through the cave?" she asked.

I shook my head. It was too small for her.

"Can you go to Faith and lead her back to us?"

I shook my head again. I couldn't. I'd never be able to navigate my way back through the cave. Even if somehow I could have convinced Veevy to guide me through it — and I had no idea how to do that — there was a good chance even Veevy didn't know where Faith was.

Bernice and I sank into some deep thinking. I gnawed the pen.

"I'll find her!" Alex said, standing and raising his fist over his head.

"You just sit, Mr. Wao," Bernice said firmly. "I don't need you lost on top of everything else."

Alex sat back down on the sand. "Yes, ma'am," he said glumly.

I can think of only one way to find Faith and lead her back here, I wrote finally.

"Tell me," Bernice said. She looked into my eyes intently.

I need a guide, I wrote.

"A guide?" she said. "What do you mean?"

There is someone who knows where Faith is, I wrote. Someone who could lead me to her, and then lead us back.

"Who?" Bernice asked urgently. "Tell me!"

A coyote, I wrote.

# Yapping and Yowling

♦ ♦ ♦ ♦ ♦ ♦ ♦ ♦

# 25

How could I be sure, dear reader, that I would even be able to locate the coyote, much less ask him to help me? I wasn't. But I had a feeling he was around. As far as his helping me goes, well, he was the best chance I had of finding Faith. Maybe the only chance. It could do no harm to ask. One thing I had already learned about the desert is that you must make do with what little you have.

I wandered away from the *Peahen*, away from Bernice and Veevy and Alex, away into the moonlit dunes, and called out to the wild dog who was not a dog.

*"Bu-roooo!"* I howled. *"Bu-rooo-oooo!"*

I very soon came upon a patch of violet flowers. They were the first flowers I'd seen since arriving in the desert and, even though I was highly mindful of the urgency and gravity of my mission, I stopped to smell them. My eyes burned, my nose tickled. I sneezed. Then again, and again — and again and again and again! I turned and fled as if I were being attacked by a swarm of bees. I was a dozen dunes away from the mint (for surely that's what it was — *hierbabuena!* — good herb, indeed!) before the sneezing began to subside.

"Bless you," came a voice from the dark. "You haven't caught cold, I hope. The temperature really does drop out here at night, doesn't it?"

It was the coyote.

"I need your help," I said.

"Really?" said the coyote, affectedly. "How surprising!"

"Could you lead me to my master?" I said, edging nearer to his scent.

"Ooof!" the coyote said. "My goodness! What have you gotten yourself into? I mean, I don't mean to be rude — stop me if I am — but you smell —"

"It's guano," I interrupted. "From a cave I went into."

"Oh, you really must be more careful," the coyote said. "You never know what you'll find in caves out here."

He had *that* right.

"I don't want to seem presumptuous," the coyote said, "but I am curious. Perhaps you could explain how is it that you can understand me? I mean, after all, you're a *dog*, aren't you?"

"I don't really know," I said.

"That you're a *dog*?"

"No. How I can understand you."

"Yes, I suppose it would be a bit much to expect from you," the coyote said. "Insight, I mean. You being a *dog* and all."

"It developed on its own," I said.

"Oh, I didn't imagine that you were self-taught!" the coyote said. "Such a bizarre notion! Perish the thought! Especially with you being a *dog*! But now I'm being repetitive."

I did not like the way he kept saying dog. He would pause slightly just before he said the word, and his voice would drop as he intoned it. That's why I keep italicizing it. There was something in the way he said it that made me think of Harry Swift.

"We've been separated," I said. "We would like to get back together again."

"Naturally," the coyote said. "Togetherness is nice."

"We're a pack," I said. "Don't you have a pack?"

"Let's leave me out of this, shall we?" said the coyote with a hint of a growl in his voice. "Let's stay with you. You and your pack. Please go on. It's fascinating. You say you and these humans are a pack, is that right?"

I could feel a blush of anger rising to my face. But I fought it down. I needed the coyote. I took a deep breath and went on.

"Yes, we're a pack, and it's no good when your pack gets separated. You must know that. We're not so different."

"You are a *dog*!" the coyote snarled. "You are *nothing* like me. I am *free*." Then he paused. He cleared his throat. When he spoke again, his voice had regained its supercilious air. "But I do not wish to talk about myself. I'd much rather hear about you. Please, tell me more."

"Why won't you help me?" I asked.

"We need to eat."

"Who needs to eat?"

"*We* do," the coyote said. The snarl was back in his voice.

"There are plenty of rabbits around," I said.

"Not enough," the coyote said. "In the desert, there is never enough. Especially with your friend around. The skinny one. Is she sick or something?"

"If you don't help us, we'll have to stay here," I said.

"Precisely," the coyote said.

"And we'll need to eat," I said.

"Yes! But you will find nothing!"

"But we already have!" I said. "Hares! Plenty of them!"

"You should tell her to stop that!" the coyote snarled. "She's killing more than she needs! She's upsetting the balance!"

"But it's her instinct. She's descended from

desert dogs. She's a rabbit courser. She can't help it."

"She must stop! There are too many predators here already! And not nearly enough prey! You must tell her to stop!"

"I can't."

"Why not?" the coyote said, with a blast of his nostrils.

"I don't know where she is," I said. Superciliously.

"Pity," said the coyote.

"If you help me find my master," I said, "and then help us to rejoin the others, we will leave the desert."

I heard the coyote grumbling to himself.

"Do you promise you will leave?" he growled finally.

"I promise," I said. (Though without fuel, dear reader, I admit I had no idea how.)

"This way," the coyote said gruffly.

♦ ♦ ♦

We did not actually travel together. The coyote remained at a distance, out of sight. I trained my nose on his scent, and did my best to keep up. Coyotes move swiftly.

"What have you got against dogs anyway?" I asked, huffing and puffing.

"Me? Nothing, nothing," the coyote said. "Superb creatures. If you like puppies."

"What do you mean?" I asked.

"Not a thing. Forget I said it."

"Do you think dogs act like puppies?" I asked.

"Do you?" the coyote replied.

"They act like dogs," I said.

"Precisely."

"Where have you seen them before?" I asked. "Dogs, I mean."

"Oh, I know what you mean," the coyote said.

"Have you ever spoken to one before?" I asked.

"Certainly, certainly," the coyote said. "None ever answered. None before you ever seemed to understand Yowl."

"Your language isn't really very different from most dog languages, you know," I said.

"Is that a fact?" the coyote said. "I've always thought that you all were just yapping."

"I imagine, to most dogs, your language would just sound like yowling," I said.

The coyote snorted.

"I smelled you before," I said. "I followed your scent. But it kept disappearing."

The coyote snickered.

"You were leading us in circles, weren't you?" I asked.

The coyote just snickered louder and never answered.

On we went, over countless dunes, under countless stars. My legs ached from walking in the deep sand, my heart, from yearning. At one point, a rattlesnake slithered by.

*"Hsss,"* it said, sibilantly. It reminded me of Veevy.

"Which of the orangeheads is your master?" the coyote asked. "Or is it the boy?"

"The girl," I said, sidestepping the snake.

"Why?" the coyote asked. "I mean to say, why do dogs have masters? Can't they hunt? Can't they scavenge?"

"Lorl — that's the skinny dog — she has a master," I said. "And she hunts. You saw her. And I spent my puppyhood scavenging."

"Then why?" the coyote asked.

"My master is my friend," I said.

"Once I saw a master beating his dog," the coyote said.

I sighed. "I've seen that happen, too. Too many times. I guess not all masters consider their dogs their friends."

"What's your name?" the coyote asked.

"Grumph," I said. "Yours?"

"I don't like to talk about myself," he said.

Suddenly, there was the mound of stones and the little rocket ship — the *Lulu*. Beside it was a round, orange, silken lump and a skinny, ever-watchful whippet.

"Thank you," I said to my invisible guide.

But his scent had vanished.

# The Good Herb

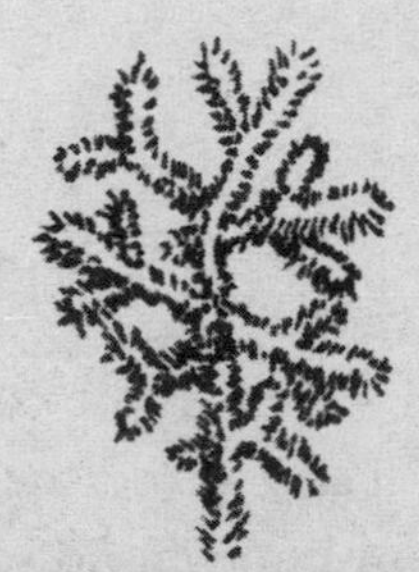

♦ ♦ ♦ ♦ ♦ ♦ ♦ ♦ ♦ ♦ ♦ ♦ ♦ ♦ ♦ ♦ ♦

# 26

"Grumph! Grumph! Grumph!" Daphne said. Oh, how I love to hear her say my name with her Arf accent!

Her barking roused Faith, and then there was laughing and yapping as we all ran to meet each other. Once I was in noseshot, however, their giddiness passed.

"Oh, Eddie!" Faith said, pinching her nose. "Whew-ee!"

"Look what the cat dragged in!" Daphne added.

"All right, all right," I said. "What do you suggest I do? I can't exactly take a bath in the middle of the desert."

"I'm sorry, widdle wuppler," Faith said with a

smile. She approached me and scratched me on a spot on my snout that didn't appear to have too much guano. She kept her nose pinched.

"I found your mother," I said.

"Mama?" she said with a gasp. "Where?"

"Not far from here. She's with your friend. In the *Peahen*." I could not translate Alex into Arf, and I'm not entirely sure I got "peahen" right. I think I actually said "cotton ball."

"She's in the *what*?" Faith asked.

"In the *rocket*," I said.

She still didn't understand, so I scratched out the shape of her rocket ship with my claw in the sand.

"Oh!" Faith squealed. "The *Peahen*!"

I nodded.

"Is she furious?" Faith said, nibbling her lower lip.

I shrugged. "I can't tell," I said. "But she sent me to fetch you."

"Then let's get going," Faith said.

She stuffed her things — her canteen, Hector's

book, some *chicles*, and a round tin container I had never seen before — into her pack, then rolled up the parachute and tied it around her waist.

**¡Listos!** ***(Spanish): Ready!***

"*¡Listos!*" she said.

I called out to my guide. He didn't answer. I couldn't smell him, either. I howled again. No answer.

I'd been duped.

"What are you saying?" Faith asked as I howled. I guess she hadn't yet learned Yowl.

I suppose I should have told her then and there that our best hope of getting back to Bernice and Alex was now effectively dashed. But I didn't. There seemed no real point in alarming her. I decided I would just lead the way as if I knew it.

♦ ♦ ♦

There were times, dear reader, when I felt that I was dead on target, and then others when I was sure I had hopelessly and forever given us over to the desert's savage tides. We happened upon more than a few hares along the way, which, in an admirable show of sensitivity and self-restraint, Daphne allowed to live. As we passed a particular cactus for the eighth time (it looked for all the world like Pooh), I felt certain we were going in circles.

But then I noticed movement behind the Pooh cactus. I saw a shadowy form slithering along amid the needles. Daphne spotted it, too, and slipped into coursing mode. She growled and the creature behind the cactus hissed.

*"Hsss!"* it said in Mew.

It was Veevy, *la gata violeta*. She must have followed me. Daphne growled and coiled to pounce.

**la gata violeta** *(Spanish): the violet cat*

"She's a friend," I said to her. "Please don't chase her down and kill her."

"It's her!" Veevy said, spying Faith. "It's my master's child!"

"Oh, widdle woozie," Faith cooed, spying the cat. "Psst, psst, psst, widdle kidder koo."

Veevy approached us in wide, swooping curves. It was as if she was walking through an invisible wood — avoiding trees that were not there.

When she finally reached us, she nuzzled up to Faith's outstretched hand and guided it up over her back.

*"Hrrrrr,"* Veevy purred loudly. Her posterior rose and her tail stiffened.

I watched Faith closely. She hadn't yet noticed who it was she was stroking. She was probably deceived by the way the night gave everything a bluish cast. But then Veevy looked up at her, the moonlight sparkling in her eyes. One of them brown, the other, green.

"Veevy!" Faith shrieked. "Veevy!"

Faith reached for her but Veevy slithered away, weaving around and between Faith's legs, purring and grazing her body against Faith's shins. Clearly she preferred attention on her own terms. That's one of the differences between cats and dogs. Dogs will take any strokes they can get. Cats pick and choose.

"Same old Veevy!" Faith said, grinning. She crouched and stroked her cat's back. "Criminitaly! You surely are a mess!"

She plucked twigs and burrs and cactus needles

from Veevy's scraggly fur. The desert had really done a job on her coat. It had gnarled it and snarled it and torn out whole tufts of it. It had also cut her nose and scratched her around the eyes and taken a bite out of her left ear.

"Oh, Veevy," Faith purred as she preened. "I missed you." She looked over at me and asked, "How do you think she got all the way out here?"

I was still unwilling to venture a guess.

Veevy crawled up onto Faith's lap and Faith massaged between her ears. The cat melted. She closed her eyes and stretched out her forepaws.

"I remember once," Faith said as she rubbed, "she dragged a dead bird into the kitchen and Mama just screamed! Veevy ran out the door and we didn't see her for over a week. Then one day she showed up at Babbo's shop. She followed him home just like nothing had happened. Babbo was so happy. He sat with her in his lap all evening, petting her." Faith stopped and kissed Veevy on the crown. "The next day, she brought in another bird."

*"Choof!"* I said abruptly. *"Raboo."*

**Choof!**
***(Bowwow):***
***Ah-choo!***

**Raboo**
***(Arf):***
***Excuse me***

**Baroof**
*(Arf):*
*Bless you*

**Mwowr**
*(Mew):*
*Bless you*

**Hur-rark!**
*(Arf):*
*This way!*

*"Salud,"* Faith said.

*"Baroof,"* Daphne said.

*"Mwowr,"* Veevy added.

*"Choof!"* I sneezed again. *"Choof!"*

"You haven't caught cold, have you?" Faith asked.

*"Choooof!"* I said so strongly that Veevy leapt off Faith's lap and darted into a patch of flowers.

A patch of *violet* flowers. The *hierbabuena*! Good herb after all!

I took a deep breath and let the mint's pollen fill my nostrils. My eyes felt as if sand had blown into them. My nose itched. And I sneezed again: *"Choo-choo-choo-CHOOOF!"* I shook my head and my flews flapped.

*"Hur-rark!"* I barked and ran toward what I was sure was the same patch of purple-blossomed mint I'd passed before, just after leaving the *Peahen*.

"What is it?" Faith yelled, running after me. Daphne fell in behind her.

When I reached the mint patch, I just kept going, lifting my nose up and sniffing for tea tree oil in the breeze.

*"Mlow!"* Veevy said, jumping out of the mint.

**Mlow!**
***(Mew):***
***Wait!***

The four of us ran as fast as our fourteen legs could carry us until finally I sniffed a familiar scent — just a whiff at first, then it grew stronger. There was no mistaking its foul, musty odor. It wasn't tea tree oil. It was the scent of scoundrels.

# Yellow Eyes

♦ ♦ ♦ ♦ ♦ ♦ ♦ ♦ ♦ ♦ ♦

# 27

I knew then, dear reader, why the coyote had stranded me, for lying in loose formation around the *Peahen,* in what I could only assume was some sort of deathwatch, was a whole pack of coyotes, my guide among them. I couldn't pick him out exactly, but my nose told me he was there.

**Ba-ba-ra-ra!** *(Arf): Intruders!*

*"Ba-ba-ra-ra!"* Daphne barked. *"Ba-ba-ra-ra!"*

The coyotes jumped to their feet. They were a nasty-looking bunch — their grizzled fur knurled and jagged, their yellow eyes blazing, their fangs bared and malicious. And I'd thought street dogs were scraggly.

"Shoo, coyotes!" Faith yelled. "Shoo! Shoo!"

"Faith?" It was Bernice's voice. It came from inside the ship.

"Mama!" Faith yelled. "Stay inside! There are coyotes out here!"

"We know!" Alex screamed. "Why do you think we're in here!"

Daphne ran at one of the coyotes. The coyote lowered its head, curled its lip. Its back arched so severely that its hind legs nearly overtook its forelegs. Daphne's ears flattened. Her tail hooked in. She snapped and snapped and snapped. Knowing the ferocity of Daphne's verbal attacks firsthand, I was unsurprised when the coyote suddenly uncurled his lip, whined, and discreetly slipped away, its tail between its legs.

Veevy picked out another of the pack. She sprung at it so suddenly that the poor thing froze. Veevy's bared claws pierced the beast's nose — a tender spot. The coyote yelped like a pup and shook Veevy off with a snap of its head. Veevy was undeterred. She lunged again, scratching the coyote's ear with a mighty swipe of her forepaw. The coyote let out a heartrending yowl. Veevy recoiled, hissing. Her eyes gleamed. The coyote spun away, tripping over itself in its rush to escape.

I admit, I was surprised. The story usually goes the other way around — you know, dog chases cat. I had a pretty good idea then how Veevy had lost that notch from her ear, and how she'd managed to stay alive in the desert. This was no ordinary house cat.

Faith rushed into the fray as well. She whooped and hollered and hurled warning stones into the sand. In short order, she and Daphne and Veevy had dispatched the entire band of malingerers to the desert, yellow eyes and all.

**mêlée** *(French): confused battle*

And what of me, dear reader? What role did I play in this little *mêlée*? Obviously, seeing as I can so clearly relate the daring exploits of my colleagues, you can probably deduce that I was in a rather, shall we say, *neutral* position during all of this. That is to say, since I can describe the battle, it can probably be reasonably assumed that I did not actually engage in it.

Well, yes. This is true. I've never really been one to assert myself physically. My bark has always been worse than my bite.

I opted instead for sniffing out my would-be

guide, the supercilious coyote, who, as the coyotes' ringleader, also sat conveniently out of harm's way, high on a dune above the battlefield. Like his brethren, he was scraggly and scrawny, his eyes, a flaming yellow. Like Veevy, he had lost a bit of his left ear.

"Hello, Grumph," he said, smirking.

"You deceived me," I said.

"Well," he said, "we coyotes have a certain reputation to live up to."

"I don't understand," I said.

"Of course you don't," the coyote said.

"I thought coyotes didn't harm people anyway," I said.

"Oh, we don't, we don't," the coyote said. "But if they should happen to wander out into the desert and, from irrational fear of us, lock themselves away — without food, without water — who could blame us for hanging around?" He grinned.

As fiendish as his remark was, I couldn't help but grin back.

"I was wondering whether you'd be leaving

now," he said, "if you don't think it impertinent my inquiring?"

"If we can," I said, and smirked.

"Yes, of course," he said, with a slight snicker. He rose to his feet. "No hard feelings, I hope."

"None," I said. "We all have to follow our noses."

"True enough," he said, then lit out like a shot.

Having now done my bit in repelling the band of marauders, I scooted triumphantly down into the breach and rejoined my pack.

# I Feel It

♦ ♦ ♦ ♦ ♦ ♦ ♦ ♦

# 28

"You're not mad?" Faith said between her mother's kisses. "I thought you'd be mad!"

"No, no!" Bernice cried. "No, sweetheart! I'm just so glad you're okay!" Then she squeezed Faith so hard Faith's gum popped out of her mouth.

Finally Bernice released her and held her at arm's length. "I'm sorry I didn't believe you," she said. Tears soaked both their faces.

Faith smiled a patient smile. "That's okay, Mama. I know it's hard for you to believe in stuff like this."

"Your father —" Bernice began. She wiped her face with her sleeve as I'd so often heard her scold Faith for doing. "Babbo would have been so proud of you," she said. Her lower lip trembled.

Drawn perhaps by their emotion, or maybe just by the salt of their tears, Daphne approached them and nosed her way up into Bernice's face. I winced. Daphne obviously did not yet know with whom she was dealing. But to my astonishment, Bernice gave her a light rub on the neck! She even said, "Good girl," in a soft, sweet voice!

I was stunned. After all, Daphne is a dog.

And then, dear reader, Bernice turned to me.

"Edison," she said softly. She opened her arms as if bidding me to come. I hung my head low, out of instinct, I suppose, and crept cautiously toward her. When I reached her, she wrapped her arms around my shoulders and hugged me. I do not lie, dear reader — *she hugged me*. Despite my being a dog, despite all that had happened between us in the past, despite, even, that I wore a hardened shell of guano and stunk to high heaven — despite it all, she hugged me. I felt her wet cheek against my neck. Her embrace seemed heavy, heartfelt, human. Then, into my fur, she spoke.

"Thank you, Eddie," she said. She swallowed hard, then added, *"Lo siento."*

*Lo siento,* dear reader, translates into English as "I'm sorry," but it means more than that. It is not just an apology. It's also an acknowledgment of feeling, of empathy, of compassion. Literally, it means "I feel it."

I could tell that Bernice felt it. Her chest heaved and her limbs shuddered. I put a forepaw on her back and carefully patted.

*"Grumph muroo-oo,"* I said.

"He said *lo siento* back, Mama," Faith said.

*"Yee-owr urr mwar!"* Veevy said.

**Grumph muroo-oo**
***(Bowwow): I feel it, too***

♦ ♦ ♦

**Yee-owr urr mwar!**
***(Mew): The evil one has changed!***

"See?" Alex said to Faith. "I set it up and I fixed it. Its fins were all banged up and its side was all dented. I found the rubber mallet and pounded them out."

"She's not an 'it,' " Faith said indignantly. "She's a 'she.' "

"Well, she doesn't have any more fuel," Alex said. "It's gone."

Faith just smiled. "These things happen," she said.

"Well, then, I guess we walk," Bernice said. "We're bound to find somebody eventually."

"No," Faith said. "Blast-off, T minus ten minutes."

Alex, Bernice, and I looked at her. Daphne and Veevy didn't.

"How?" Bernice asked.

Faith fished around inside her backpack. "I don't know if it'll work," she said, "but it's all we have." She pulled out the round tin container — the one I'd never seen before. "It's from the *Lulu,*" she said.

I sniffed the container. Olives and garlic.

As Faith ran through her systems check with Alex, Bernice sat on a rock beside me, nibbling on her lower lip.

"I guess the world will know now," she said. She looked over at Alex, who was calling out "Check!" after each item Faith read aloud. "He's seen the rocket fly and he's seen you write. And that woman — that French woman — she saw the blast off. They'll open their mouths and, before you know it, everyone and their dog will be at our door." She looked down at me. "If you'll pardon the expression."

*"Urbruff,"* I said.

**Urbruff**

***(Bowwow): Don't worry***

"Come on, Mama!" Faith yelled from the cockpit. "T minus two minutes!"

Bernice climbed — willingly this time — into the *Peahen,* while I corralled Daphne. She had just extinguished the life of yet another poor desert hare. It hung from her jaws.

"Oh, Lorl," I said with a sigh.

*"Mlal mlalt mlah-mlah,"* she said. (There's no translation, dear reader. I don't know what she said. She was speaking with her mouth full.)

We boarded and took our places under the red pine chairs. Alex sat on the floor between us. Veevy just kept circling around us.

"I don't know," she was saying. "There's a lot of deadweight. A lot of deadweight and precious little fuel."

"Commencing countdown!" Faith said. "Ten . . . nine . . . eight . . ."

"I pray the fuel's still good," I heard Bernice mutter.

"Seven . . . six . . . five . . . four . . ."

"I hope there's enough," Alex said.

"Three . . . two . . . one . . ."

"Good-bye, rabbits," Daphne said sadly.

"Ignition . . . blast off!"

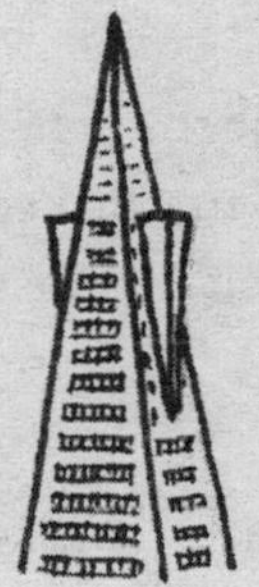

# ¡Perfecto!

♦ ♦ ♦ ♦ ♦ ♦ ♦ ♦ ♦

# 29

Even though the *Peahen* outsized the *Lulu* considerably, and the crew surely outweighed any passengers the *Lulu* may have transported (and I'm still not guessing who that might have been), the *Lulu*'s fuel was still enough to fire the *Peahen* high into the predawn sky in the ripsnorting manner to which she'd become accustomed.

"How are you going to find our way back?" Bernice asked Faith. "It's dark. How will you navigate?"

Faith looked at Bernice nervously. "I didn't think of that," she said. "Are you mad?"

"No sweat," Alex said calmly. "We'll simply use celestial navigation. You know — follow the stars."

"Do you know how to do that, Alex?" Bernice asked skeptically.

"Sure," he said. "It's a cinch." He pressed his nose up to the porthole. Stars flickered by like sparks. "There's the Dog Star," Alex said. "Bear starboard, Faith."

"Huh?" Faith said.

"Go right a little."

"Check," Faith said.

The *Peahen* shifted course and sailed onward into the night sky, past the stars that guided her. Just exactly who was listening to those stars, Alex or the *Peahen*, I can't say. All I'm sure of is that after a very short time — just as short a time as our first flight had taken, which was short indeed — Alex yelled, "I see it! San Francisco!"

I rushed to see, but Alex shoved me out of the way with his forearm.

"My turn!" he said, scowling.

*"Grumph rowroof rr woof Grumph!"* I said.

"I like your words, Eddie," Faith said, and patted my crown.

Alex's scowl faded. *"Dui bu qui, dui bu qui,"* he said, then added, "Please, after you."

This from a boy! Amazing. Our little voyage

**Grumph rowroof rr woof Grumph!**
***(Arf): I don't like it when you push me!***

**Dui bu qui**
***(Chinese): I'm sorry***

had produced quite a few small miracles — and it had not ended yet.

I scanned the scene below. I saw a radio tower with blinking red lights atop a tall hill. I saw the Golden Gate Bridge, which I recognized from snapshots Faith had shown me long ago in Mexico. I saw the tall, glass towers — the *rascacielos*. One was very pointy, like the tip of a pencil. It was the pyramid!

**rascacielos** *(Spanish): skyscrapers*

"I see the pyramid!" I reported.

"The what?" Faith said.

She didn't know "pyramid" in Arf. I tried another tack.

"The tall, white pointy building," I said. "By the bookstore."

"The pyramid?"

"Faith?" Bernice said, somewhat perplexed. "Are you *answering* him?"

"I'm real busy right now, Mama," Faith said. "We can talk later."

"Excuse me, Edison," Alex said. "May I look?"

Amazing.

"Yep," he said. "It's the pyramid, all right. Bear to port."

"Huh?" Faith asked.

"Left a little," Alex said.

"Roger," Faith said.

"May I see, Mr. Wao?" Bernice asked.

"Of course," said Alex and moved away from the window.

"I can see our house, Faith," Bernice said, looking out the porthole. "It's right down there."

"Let me see, Mama," Faith said.

"See?" Bernice said, pointing. "There's Telegraph Hill."

"Okay, everybody," Faith said, settling back in her seat. "Brace yourselves. We're going in."

I crawled under Bernice's chair and curled up beside Daphne. I felt her trembling with fear.

"You're shaking," she said to me.

Maybe it wasn't her.

Alex sat on Bernice's lap. Bernice placed her hand on her daughter's shoulder.

"You can do it, pumpkin," she said. "I know you can."

I could hear in her voice absolute trust, absolute faith.

And I had no fear.

♦ ♦ ♦

Bernice unlocked the hatch and pushed it open. Veevy slipped by her.

*"Hrrr myorrrr!"* she purred.

**Hrrr myorrrr!** *(Mew): Nice landing!*

"Well?" Faith asked her mother. "Where are we?"

Bernice just turned, said, "Come see!" and stepped down from the ship. Alex peered outside and smiled, then climbed down, too. Faith was next, with me hot on her heels.

Outside, hugging Bernice on our back stoop, stood Hector.

*"¡Perfecto, mi hija!"* he called to Faith. *"¡Perfecto!"*

**¡Perfecto!** *(Spanish): Perfect!*

# Bernice's Doing

# 30

The next day was a school day. Bernice decided to accompany Faith to Double Happiness Elementary, and suggested I go along, too.

"I want to be there when Alex drops the bomb," she said.

Madame Moucher had already threatened to go to the authorities with charges against Bernice for what she called "a clear case of dognapping," and for recklessly endangering her life — and her whippet's — with "an unguided missile."

"My only hope is that the story is so wild no one will ever believe either of them," Bernice said to me as we neared the school. "At least Madame Moucher didn't see you write."

*"Urbruff,"* I said.

◆ ◆ ◆

The bomb dropped during circle time.

"Yes, Alexander," Ms. Ng said. "Would you like to share something with the group?"

Alex quickly lowered his hand. "Yes, thank you, Ms. Ng," he said. "I went up in Faith's rocket ship!"

Bernice sighed from her chair in the corner.

"I see," Ms. Ng said, nodding. "You say you flew in Faith's rocket ship, is that right?"

"Yeah!" Alex said. He was fairly bursting right out of his skin. "And her dog *writes*!"

The children snickered.

Alex scowled. "It's true!"

Faith peeked over at Bernice. Bernice extended her index finger and pressed it to her lips. "Sssh!" it meant. Faith winked.

"You're saying that Faith's dog can write, is that right, Alex?" Ms. Ng said.

"Yeah, right!" Jeffrey laughed.

Alex jumped to his feet. "He can! It's true!"

The children laughed again, harder this time.

"Could you please be seated while we're talking, Alex?" Ms. Ng asked.

Alex whirled around to face Faith. "Tell them!" he urged. "Tell them it's true!"

Faith looked over again at her mother. At this point all Bernice needed to do was signal again and Faith would have denied all of Alex's claims. She needed only to give the slightest shake of her head to escape sheer and utter pandemonium.

But she didn't. Instead, she wrung her hands. She bit her lip. She was making a hard decision. I imagine it went like this: should she tell Faith to speak the truth and in so doing turn our lives upside down, or should she ask her to lie?

Well, dear reader, what would you have done?

"It's true," Bernice said, standing. "What he is saying is true."

She sighed a deep sigh, rolled her eyes, and joined the circle.

# Epilogue: The Excavation Complete

In the months following, pandemonium did indeed descend upon our house.

In an effort to handle the steady flow of hucksters, hoodwinkers, backslappers, and bamboozlers, Bernice sold her folk arts shop and took on the full-time role of personal manager to Faith and me.

"I'll keep the wolves at bay," she told us.

She spent her days slamming down the phone and slamming the door and saying things like "You must be out of your cotton-picking mind!" or "You've got more dollars than sense!" It seemed a job she was born to do.

Faith showed little interest in the hubbub going on all around her — the television cameras, the reporters, the crowds, the National Aeronautics and Space Administration. She was far too engrossed in her various inventions to be distracted. On her drawing board were several improvements for the *Peahen* (including the installation of seat belts, a reserve fuel tank, and a navigational system), designs for a seafaring vessel (dubbed the *Seahen*), and a canteen for dogs.

Of course, she also had playing and singing and reading to do, and friends to be with (including your faithful narrator). She kept occasional company with Alex, but no more than she did with Alexandra, or Pouen, or Noe, or any of her other friends at school. She spent a great deal of time answering the heaps of letters that were delivered each day in big canvas sacks. Mostly the letters were from children, many of them written in tongues Faith did not understand. I translated them for her in the beginning, but after a while she began doing a lot of it herself.

Alex originated and appointed himself president of the very first Luisa Faith Urquhart-Brindisi fan club. Through its monthly newsletter, *Faith in the Peahen,* he has helped to keep the youth of the world updated on Faith's latest exploits, and also continually reminds them of the crucial role he played in the historic flight that catapulted Faith to fame. By the way, he adopted a Mexican electric dog of his own — Murl, the mutt from the jail — and began his own series of rocket experiments on the roof of his apartment building in Chinatown.

Madame Moucher not only failed to convince the authorities of any wrongdoing on Bernice's part, but, what's more, she found herself with a show dog who no longer wished to show. Whenever Madame approached her with, say, toenail clippers or nail polish or bay leaf perfume, Daphne would just snap and snap and snap and snap until Madame finally just threw her hands up and said, *"Nom de chien!"*

**Nom de chien!** *(French): My goodness!; literally, name of the dog*

Daphne asked me if I could help her find a place in which she might course rabbits. In San Francisco, the closest I could find was greyhound racing. The track's brochure claimed that rabbits were used as lures. That was enough for Daphne. Together, we convinced Madame to enter her in a race. When the big day came, I was quite surprised and amused to find that the lures were actually mechanical — electric hares! (I must remember to read brochures more carefully.)

After the race, I expected Daphne to be furious, but instead, she asked to be signed up for another heat.

"The chase is more fun than the kill anyway," she said with a shrug.

It's a good thing she's a sight hound.

I did my best to see her as often as possible. Though I have been very busy writing this story — the end of which, dear reader, you're just now nearing — I've still found time to compose poems for her. I've taken to writing them in Arf to save me from having to translate them as I recite. Lately, Daphne has been asking me to go through the poems with her word by word, explaining which word represents which bark, and which letter, which sound. She's even tried to do a little writing herself and, in such, has shown a rudimentary grasp of snoutmanship. Her S's especially are exemplary.

Veevy moved back in with us, of course, and had a very tough time readjusting to domestic life. Her bird-killing prowess had become so sharpened by her stay in the desert that she refused to eat anything as dull and lifeless as kibbles. Bernice soon tired of finding dead birds around the house and, much to Veevy's chagrin, hooked a bell to the cat's collar. One day, as I watched the now well-groomed, purplish (Faith would say bluish) kitty cursing and clawing at her collar, the bell madly tinkling away, I wrote a little rhyme:

Valentina
Vladimirovna
Nikolayeva
Tereshkova
Tell me how you
Found a way to
Manage to strike a
Match to light the
Fuse?

As time has passed, Bernice has become more and more tolerant of my presence. Oh, she still cringes at some of my more beastly habits. She seems especially unaccepting, for instance, of the sorts of things I choose to pick up off the ground and eat. And she has never truly become accustomed to my scent, whether bathed or unbathed. Lately, she has resorted to dousing me with tea tree oil.

Hector continues teaching his classes at the university. He's a teacher of anthropology, by the way. Anthropology is the study of man. Imagine my surprise then when one day he asked me to come as a "special guest speaker."

"The story of humankind," he explained to his class, "would be incomplete without the story of dogkind."

Faith tagged along to translate.

As for me, well, I have been under almost constant siege by reporters and scientists and publishers and the like, all wanting me to tell how I came to be able to read and write, or how I feel about human beings and the way they treat us, or what dog food I eat. At times, it has been a nuisance. I can't write in the backyard anymore, and I've slept less — some days as little as fifteen hours.

But, I really shouldn't complain. Bernice has done an excellent job of keeping life fairly normal around the house, and I'm allowed to go out whenever I like, provided I am accompanied by a grim-looking group of men in dark glasses whom Bernice calls "security." I'm allowed to make routine trips to the city's many bookstores, libraries, and *carnicerías.* I often visit or am visited by Daphne, Murl, and Yark (who was finally remembered by the house sitter, by the way, and reclaimed). And sometimes Bernice allows in certain people of what she calls "great stature and prestige" who have asked to meet me. They come from all over the world to rub my belly and say "Good dog" in many different languages. (For example, a woman from Istanbul said, *"Iyi köpek."*) I have also traveled extensively throughout the world, and in first class — not baggage.

**Iyi köpek**
***(Turkish): Good dog***

One of these trips took us back to San Cristóbal de las Casas, where a stone statue in my image had been erected at my birthplace on Avenida 5 de Mayo. Yip was there for the unveiling.

"There's one dog that's safe from parvo!" he quipped.

"And taxis," I added.

We spent that night in our home on Avenida Pichucalco, and as I lay in Bernice's fuchsia bed, gnawing on a bone Faith had failed to find, a reporter scaled the courtyard wall. I knew he was a reporter because he started right off with the questions.

"So how does it feel to be the most famous pooch in the world?" he asked in English. He had an Australian accent.

I didn't answer him, dear reader, mostly because Bernice has expressly forbidden me to ever answer reporters, but also because I had no pen and paper handy. But I have since thought a lot about his question, and have come to realize that fame hasn't really changed my outlook on life in any truly significant way at all. I mean, attention from strangers is pleasant — in small doses — and I'm awfully glad that my stories have become books. I'm especially glad to have been able to share my story with you, dear reader, and if it took fame to make that happen, well, then it surely can't be all bad.

But the truth is, a dog doesn't really need the love of the whole world to be happy. For me, anyway, Faith is enough. (Though *shumei*, from time to time, is nice.)

♦ ♦ ♦

Well, that's just about it. Every bone dug up, dusted off, and gnawed. All, that is, save one:

I understand that Harry Swift, formerly noted animal behaviorist and author, has opened his own little nightclub in San Francisco and performs cabaret there nightly to a packed house. I've read that he's quite good and would love to go and hear him. Unfortunately, dogs are not allowed.

**The End**

# Glossary

♦ ♦ ♦ ♦ ♦ ♦ ♦ ♦

**A Faithita, con cariño Señora Tiza y la clase 4° nivel.** (Spanish): To little Faith, with affection, Senora Tiza and the fourth-grade class.
**à la** (French): in the manner of
**Adieu** (French): Good-bye
**Ai ya!** (Chinese): Wow!
**¡Alta!** (Spanish): Stop!
**aquí** (Spanish): here
**arco iris** (Spanish): rainbow
**armario** (Spanish): armoire; wardrobe
**Aroo bu?** (Bowwow): What's your name?
**Aroo cur?** (Bowwow): Aren't you an electric dog?
**¡Ay!** (Spanish): Oh!
**Ba-ba-ra!** (Arf): Intruder!
**Ba-ba-ra-ra** (Arf): Intruders!

**Baroo** (Bowwow): Excuse me
**Baroof** (Arf): Bless you
**¡Basta!** (Spanish): Enough!
**belabete** (Spanish): beet
**bella somma** (Italian): pretty penny
**bistec** (Spanish): beefsteak
**bock** (Bowwow): parrot
**boda** (Spanish): wedding
**Bravissimo!** (Italian): Excellent!; Bravo!
**Bu Grumph** (Bowwow): My name is Grumph
**Bu-roo!** (Bowwow): I'm here!
**Buena suerte** (Spanish): Good luck
**Bueno** (Spanish): Good
**Buenos días** (Spanish): Good morning
**¡Buenos tardes, Señor Paniagua!** (Spanish): Good afternoon, Mr. Paniagua!
**Cálmate** (Spanish): Calm down
**cálmate, mi cielo** (Spanish): calm down, my sky, or heaven (a term of endearment).
**Canis familiaris** (Latin): domesticated dog
**cannoli** (Italian): a pastry filled with cream and ricotta cheese

**carnicería** (Spanish): butcher shop
**carnitas** (Spanish): roasted pork nuggets glazed in fat drippings
**chicles** (Spanish): chewing gum
**chistosa** (Spanish): funny
**Choof!** (Bowwow): Ah-choo!
**ciao** (Italian): good-bye
**cocodrilo** (Spanish): crocodile
**colíbri** (Spanish): hummingbird
**Comment allez-vous, Madame?** (French): How do you do, Madame?
**conejillo de Indias** (Spanish): guinea pig
**conejito** (Spanish): bunny
**corriente** (Spanish): common; also, current, as in electrical current
**¡Cuidado!** (Spanish): Be careful!
**cúmbias** (Spanish): popular dance songs of Mexico
**De nada** (Spanish): You're welcome
**Dui bu qui** (Chinese): I'm sorry
**dulcería** (Spanish): candy shop
**Ee-row!** (Arf): I'm here!
**Eeroo snap!** (Arf): I'm a whippet!

***El conejito andarín*** (Spanish): *The Runaway Bunny*
**enchanté** (French): enchanted; pleased to meet you
**equipaje** (Spanish): luggage
**estufa** (Spanish): stove
**Fichez le camp!** (French): Beat it!
**frágil** (Spanish): fragile
**Froo garf** (Arf): It's the pill
**fruffruff** (Bowwow): little parrot
**fur** (Bowwow): yard dog
**¡Gracias!** (Spanish): Thank you!
**Grazie** (Italian): Thank you
**Groo-oorr!** (Arf): Run!
**Grourgurg!** (Arf): Earthquake!
**Grumph garfroo** (Bowwow): I'll check on you
**Grumph groo** (Bowwow): I'm fine
**Grumph groomph** (Bowwow): I'm not surprised
**Grumph muroo** (Bowwow): I'm sorry
**Grumph muroo-oo** (Bowwow): I'm sorry, too
**Grumph rowroof rr woof Grumph!** (Arf): I don't like it when you push me!
**Grumph rroof-roof** (Arf): I love you

**harpa** (Spanish): harp
**hierbabuena** (Spanish): mint; literally, good herb
**hipos** (Spanish): the hiccups
**Hoo-ark!** (Bowwow): This way!
**Hoo-hooooo!** (Bowwow): Let me out!
**Hrrr** (Mew): Nice
**Hrrr myorrrr!** (Mew): Nice landing!
**Hsss, yee-owr!** (Mew): Go away, evil one!
**Hssss!** (Mew): Get lost!
**Hur-rark!** (Arf): This way!
**italiano** (Italian): Italian
**Iyi köpek** (Turkish): Good dog
**la gata violeta** (Spanish): the violet cat
**¿La raza?** (Spanish): The breed?
**Lao Shi** (Chinese): Teacher (an address of respect)
**laurel** (Spanish): bay leaf
**¡Listos!** (Spanish): Ready!
**Liu leng gou!** (Chinese): mutt; electric dog
**Lo que ella no save no les daña** (Spanish): What she doesn't know won't hurt her
**Lo siento** (Spanish): I'm sorry
**Loor!** (Arf): Please!
**Lorl ayoo!** (Bowwow): She's here!

**los angeles** (Spanish): the angels
**Mama mia!** (Italian): My goodness!; literally, my mama
**manteca** (Spanish): pig fat
**Mee-yoo** (Mew): I'm here
**mêlée** (French): confused battle
**mercado** (Spanish): market
**mi hija** (Spanish): an affectionate term for a little girl; literally, my daughter
**Mlow!** (Mew): Wait!
**Mwowr** (Mew): Bless you
**Ni hao** (Chinese): Hello
**niños** (Spanish): children
**Nom de chien!** (French): My goodness!; literally, name of the dog
**nonno** (Italian): grandfather
**Oo cur?** (Bowwow): An electric dog?
**oo ur** (Bowwow): a dog
**Oobroorr gurr yurr** (Bowwow): A lot of bones have been buried in the yard
**Ooo-rooo! Ooo-rrr!** (Yowl): I'm here! I'm hungry!
**Ow groo!** (Bowwow): That's fine!

**Ow Grumph!** (Bowwow): It's me!
**Ow owr!** (Bowwow): It's true!
**padrastro** (Spanish): stepfather
**palomas** (Spanish): doves; pigeons
**¿Pan y agua?** (Spanish): Bread and water
**¡Perfecto!** (Spanish): Perfect!
**perra** (Spanish): female dog
**pescado** (Spanish): fish
**querida** (Spanish): sweetheart; dear
**Raboo** (Arf): Excuse me
**Raboo, loor!** (Arf): Excuse me, please!
**rascacielos** (Spanish): skyscrapers
**Roo!** (Arf): Hey!
**Roo-ah bowwow ar ur bark!** (Bowwow): You're really barking up the wrong tree!
**Roo-ah Cur-Rr!** (Bowwow): You're Mexican!
**Roof** (Bowwow): Hi
**Roor!** (Bowwow): Sure!
**Rowr froo?** (Arf): Where is it?
**Rowr grull?** (Arf): Not an electric dog?
**rr** (Bowwow): land
**Ruff!** (Bowwow): Hey!

**sala** (Spanish): living room
**sale chien!** (French): dirty dog
**¡Salud!** (Spanish): Your health!
**shumei** (Chinese): pork dumplings
**¡Sí!** (Spanish): Yes!
**Sí, claro. No te preocupes** (Spanish): Sure; don't worry
**Sí, es verdad** (Spanish): Yes, it's true
**sniff** (Arf): snob
**sopa de chícharo** (Spanish): pea soup
**¿Tienes hambre?** (Spanish): Are you hungry?; literally, Do you have hunger?
**¿Un perro corriente?** (Spanish): a mutt; literally, a common dog; can also be translated as "an electric dog"
**Urbruff** (Bowwow): Don't worry
**Urf** (Bowwow): Thanks
**¡Vamonos!** (Spanish): Let's go!
**Venez ici** (French): Come here
**Veo, veo** (Spanish): I see, I see
**Yee-owr urr mwar!** (Mew): The evil one has changed!

**Yowr-rew** (Mew): About time
**Yowr-rr-rr!** (Bowwow): Yee-ouch!
**Yur-ark!** (Bowwow): Egotist!
**zapatería** (Spanish): shoe store